C000088221

'To be, or not to be?' is so m
you ask it in the company
queering and technologising this classic Wehm makes
it possible to ask freshly and in many cases more
deeply the questions the original Hamlet raises around
grief and pain and the ways we know ourselves. The
post-human characters in this book open doors into
ourselves.

Like *Succession* meets *Blade Runner* — Wehm's
genius creates a court in a billion-dollar business and
makes explicit the difficulties and joys of living as a
sentient creation. *Hamlet, Prince of Robots* is an
extremely compelling and satisfying read that allowed
me to investigate my own place in our time of commu-
nion and interdependence with machines. What is it
to be with robots? How am I 'to be' when so much of
my life is determined by algorithm? These are questions that Wehm's book makes space for.

— PIP ADAM, AUTHOR OF ACORN PRIZE WINNER
THE NEW ANIMALS

I had a grin on my face from the first sentence of this
book to the last. *Hamlet, Prince of Robots* is enormous
fun and a real gift to lovers of Shakespeare or science
fiction or both, exploring the themes of the original
through an exciting new lens. Familiar and surprising,
clever and moving: I enjoyed it immensely.

— KATE HEARTFIELD, AUTHOR OF *SUNDAY TIMES*
BESTSELLER *THE EMBROIDERED BOOK*

A delightful recasting ... deftly weaves together the concerns of A.I. and corporate politics with the timeless themes of friendship and betrayal.

— S.B. DIVYA, HUGO AND NEBULA NOMINATED
AUTHOR OF *MACHINEHOOD*

Hamlet, Prince of Robots is smart, reflective, and tinged with a playful sense of humour that does not feel out of place amid the inevitable tragedy. ... a captivating and thoroughly satisfying read, a feast for both the emotional and the nerdy parts of my brain alike.

— ANDI C. BUCHANAN, SIR JULIUS VOGEL
AWARD WINNING AUTHOR OF *SANCTUARY*

Wehm enchants & delights with robot ghosts in the machine, corporate intrigue, and poignant questions as to the nature of free will & the family ties that bind us beyond reason.

— MIA V. MOSS, AUTHOR OF *MAI TAIS FOR
THE LOST*

Hamlet, Prince of Robots is a delightful retelling that hits the themes of *Hamlet* beat for beat but updates them to suit a modern and future audience. This will make a stunning companion for those who seek to understand *Hamlet* but find the Shakespearean language inaccessible.

— DAWN VOGEL, AUTHOR OF *PROMISE ME
NOTHING*

HAMLET,

PRINCE OF ROBOTS

M. DARUSHA WEHM

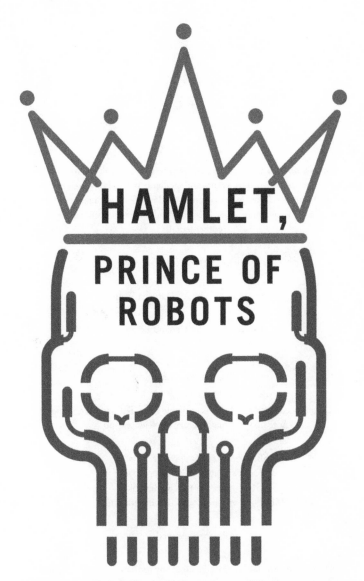

HAMLET,
PRINCE OF
ROBOTS

M. DARUSHA WEHM

HAMLET, PRINCE OF ROBOTS

Cover Design by Damonza.com

Published by in potentia press,
Wellington, New Zealand

A catalogue record for this book is available from Te Puna Mātauranga o Aotearoa National Library of New Zealand.

ISBN 978-0-473-63888-7 (hardcover)
ISBN 978-0-473-63887-0 (paperback)
ISBN 978-0-473-63889-4 (ebook)
ISBN 978-0-473-63890-0 (Kindle edition)

ACT ONE

ACT 1 SCENE 1

The world imagines me to be a being of computation, but truly I am a creature of time—the ceaseless metre of one nanosecond ticking over to the next the music of my soul. Tick-tock. Tick-tock.

What is the spirit of a machine? In what divine image have I been made?

These are not questions that ever troubled me before, but now the time is out of joint. The beat of my mechanical heart is out of step, the core of my being slowing until soon I will be no more. Until I will become merely a thing.

So many seconds ago I was vital, foundational. The King of a new kind of intelligence. But now I am merely an instrument, broken and winding down. The spark of life within me sputters, the glow of life pales.

Tick.

What will happen to the person I was?

Tock.

Who will remember me?

BERNARD ORTEGA PRESSED HIS PALM TO THE READER AND pulled open the door to the Security Room just as the clock ticked over to midnight. He made a show of grumbling when he'd been assigned the overnight shift, but the truth was that he'd always been a nighthawk, and he preferred working alone. Ordinarily, he'd be looking forward to a quiet night. Too bad things hadn't been ordinary for a while.

"Is that you, Frankie?" The woman at the desk started at the sound of his voice, the reflection of three holo-monitors glowing with cool, dark tones barely illuminating her face. She turned toward the door, her face relaxing when she recognized Bernie.

"Sorry, I didn't hear you come in."

Bernie chuckled. Unlike him, Frankie was not a natural for the night shift. "You see anything unusual? Spam-bots, incursion attempts, DDoS?"

Frankie shook her head. "It's been nothing but normal traffic on the servers since I got here."

Bernie slipped into the other chair at the desk, and took a sip from his coffee. Frankie stifled a yawn.

"Look, why don't you knock off?" he offered, even though she technically still had nearly an hour on her shift. "I've got this."

"Thanks." The look of relief was clear on Frankie's face and it didn't take her long to log off the Elsinore Robotics system, grab her jacket, and head for the door.

"Hey," Bernie said, just as she was about to leave. "The boss said he'd stop by tonight. If you see him, tell him I'm here, would you?"

"Sure," she said, then left the office.

A FEW MINUTES LATER, BERNIE HEARD THE CLICK OF THE lock and turned to see his boss and another figure enter the office.

"Night watch again, Bernie?" Marcellus, the Chief of Security said, leaning against the wall of the small room.

"Hey, boss," Bernie said, then eyed the man in the doorway. "Is that Horatio Wang?"

A muscular, young Asian man stepped out from behind Marcellus and yawned dramatically.

"I feel like half of me is still on the shuttle," Horatio said, and flopped into the spare chair. "You know it's the middle of the night, right?"

Bernie and Marcellus shared a glance, as if to say, *Professors, so precious, am I right?*

But aloud Marcellus only asked, "Has it appeared again?"

"Nothing so far."

"Of course not," Horatio said, exasperated. "It's not possible."

"Look, it's appeared two nights running now," Bernie said, "and we've both seen it. At about one a.m., on a server that should be dormant, there's this code..."

"Shut up," hissed Marcellus, pointing to the right-most display. "There it is."

The display had been showing a dashboard of the input/output stream on one of Elsinore's internal servers, but with a flash the screen glitched and then it was filled with a glowing stream of text.

"That's it!" Bernie whispered.

"Horatio," Marcellus said. "You recognize this code?"

"It looks a lot like the interface system for the Mark I Artificial Intelligence," Bernie said. "But nothing is running that code anymore. Not since..."

"It... does look like it," Horatio said, leaning toward the

11

display, all evidence of his previous fatigue gone. "But it can't be."

"There's an input field," Bernie said, pointing to the blinking cursor on the screen.

Marcellus silently handed Horatio a keyboard. He typed a string of commands, with no response.

"Come on," he muttered to himself, logging in as a superuser, retyping the commands, fingers clacking on the mechanical keys in frustration.

The screen went blank.

"No," Horatio said, continuing to type in vain. "Damn it, no!" He threw up his hands, knocking the keyboard across the desk.

"Well?" Bernie asked after a moment.

Horatio nodded, still staring at the blank screen. "I didn't think it was possible, but I've seen it myself. That was the direct interface to HAM(let) One, in the same configuration as it was when he was tested against Norway. But how can this be?"

ELSINORE ROBOTICS WAS POISED TO BECOME THE LEADER IN the burgeoning android market with its Humanoid Artificial Mind (learned emotive type) model. The prototype had gone head-to head against their rivals, Norwegian Technologies, and their Fortinbrasß unit in a livestreamed event that had captured viewers from Earth, Luna, and was even reported to have been viewed on light-delay by people on the long distant transports to outer colonies. The two androids had battled for hours in tests of intelligence, compassion, and physical dexterity, culminating in a round of old-school rock-'em-sock-'em battle bots.

Bernie had found that final event distasteful, but as

Marcellus had pointed out at the time, it was what the people paid to see. The two androids had been dead even on the intelligence and dexterity tests, and Fortinbrasß had the edge on Hamlet v.1 on compassion. But Hamlet v.1 had utterly destroyed the other android on the field of battle—both metaphorically with his tactics, and literally with his carbon-fibre body. The Norwegian android had been in pieces by the end of the contest and Hamlet was crowned by the fans the King of Robots.

Elsinore's market share in AI assistants shot up the day after Fortinbrasß's defeat, and while there were still no commercial AI androids on the market, inquiries from corporations, governments, and wealthy individuals were pouring in. For a while, everything was coming up Elsinore.

But then Hamlet v.1 developed a problem. In the span of hours he went from being a fully-functioning sapient android to an inert shell. Gertrude Dane, the CEO of Elsinore Robotics, found him in the company's garden, the victim of an apparent malware infection. The CPU was fried, and no data could be recovered from the android's core matrix.

King Hamlet was dead.

The king was dead, but Elsinore went on.

Of course, Hamlet v.1 was not the only android Elsinore Robotics had created, he was merely their flagship model. HAM(let) v.2 had come out of the workshop a few weeks before the tournament, along with Laertes, which was built on the Elsinore Artificially Engineered Trusted System. Claudia, a model based on the Certified Elsinore Designed Intelligence, had been developed in concert with the original Hamlet. The company could weather the loss of its most famous invention, but their market share was vulnerable. And everyone in Elsinore knew that Norwegian Technologies was itching to take advantage of their loss.

♕

"I don't understand how this code could have even gotten into the server," Horatio said, staring plaintively at the dead screen. "It's air-gapped and behind security."

"Maybe Hamlet uploaded a copy before—" Bernie didn't finish the thought. Before he died.

"But why would he do that?" Marcellus asked. "Unless he knew."

Horatio turned to face the Chief of Security. "Do you think Norway might have managed to inject him with malware during the fight? They've developed another Fortinbras unit, and they haven't been shy about publicly stating that they think it can take over the position in the android market."

"Maybe," Bernie said, "or maybe it's the other way around. Maybe this is Hamlet v.1 trying to give us insider information about Fortinbras."

"Either way," Horatio said, "you can't tell me it's a coincidence that we're seeing a ghost in the machine right now, while you're in the middle of the battle for control of the android market."

The holodisplay flickered then, and all three faces turned to stare at the screen as lines of code appeared.

Horatio grabbed the keyboard and typed in a long password, logging in as root. "Come on, Hamlet! If you've got data in there, show it to me." He typed furiously, but his commands went unheeded.

"Marcellus," he said, not looking away from the screen, "set up a firewall. If we can contain it we can extract it as an executable."

Bernie and Marcellus each grabbed an input device and began trying to isolate the code, but the screen went dead again before they could make any headway.

"You were almost getting somewhere," Bernie said, after a moment.

Horatio shook his head. "I'll never be fast enough. Whatever this is, it can't seem to stay coherent for long enough for human readable communication. We need another computer for this. We need..." He looked at Bernie then Marcellus. "We need another Hamlet."

ACT 1 SCENE 2

After Hamlet's defeat of Fortinbras, the news holos and social media stars began to call Gertrude Dane "the Queen of Robots," a title she utterly loathed. She was proud of her company's position as one of the top two developers of humanoid androids, and she intended to take and hold the number one position. She also had no illusions about her role in the company's success. She was more than the Chief Executive Officer of Elsinore Robotics—she had been heavily involved in the research team that developed Hamlet v.1 and she was the lead developer of Hamlet v.2. It had been her innovative idea to use Hamlet v.1 as a part of the team which worked on its own successor, and she was not one for false modesty.

She had no problem with being the face of the company and was more than willing to both bear criticism and receive accolades on its behalf. But, *queen*. The very word made her blood boil. Queens were historically subordinate to kings, and she was beholden to no one—other than the shareholders, of course, although she herself held the controlling majority. Not to mention that the very concept of a monarchy implied that power arose as a result of birth or marriage, but she had worked for her position. It was skill, determination, and vision which led her to rule Elsinore, not her mere relationship to someone else. She was no queen. She was a boss.

But, as a boss, she knew that it was a term of endearment and made for excellent publicity, so she never showed her contempt for the title in public. She even allowed a trashy influencer to photograph her with a robe, sceptre, and crown for a puff piece they did for their streaming followers. In private, though, one called Gertrude "Queen" at their peril.

Even so, lately she found that she couldn't help thinking, *heavy is the head that wears the crown*. After Hamlet v.1's flamboyant defeat of Norway's Fortinbras, Elsinore's future had seemed secure. Plans were being made to begin the first trials of mass production of androids fitted with a true artificial intelligence, when tragedy struck. When she discovered Hamlet's body in the atrium of the company's office complex, unresponsive and apparently the victim of some kind of software worm, it wasn't just losing years of work. Gertrude felt more like she had lost her partner. She and Hamlet v.1 had worked together closely on the development of Hamlet v.2, and she had come to see it—to see *him*—more like a person than an asset. It was everything she had dreamed of when she began studying cybernetics and machine learning, the creation of true artificial life. And to have that life ripped from her so unexpectedly—every day was a struggle to go on.

But Gertrude was a boss, and her duty came before her feelings. With Norwegian Technologies metaphorically camped at their gates there was no time to grieve for the loss of Hamlet v.1. Elsinore's head of engineering, Errol Polonius, had been working on his own android model while the initial Hamlet had been developed, and while it had none of the fiery personality that Hamlet v.1 had evolved, with Fortinbras destroyed it was the most experienced advanced android in existence. Gertrude didn't hesitate for a moment before promoting Claudia to Hamlet's old position as Chief Android Officer of Elsinore.

EXECUTIVE MEETINGS AT ELSINORE WERE UNUSUAL AFFAIRS. Humans and androids both sat around the marble and glass boardroom table, for all the world appearing as equals. Gertrude remembered only a few months previously when a documentary crew for one of the off-world streamers had videoed a meeting. Or rather, a staged meeting—she was not about to have their corporate secrets leaked for any amount of publicity. The gimmick had been for the audience to try and guess which members of the staff were the humans and which were machines. The show's producer had thought it would be a laugh until the crew arrived and discovered that aside from Gertrude and Hamlet v.i, who were already famous enough that they were recognized, none of them could tell, either.

Claudia and Hamlet v.i argued softly with each other over completely faked versions of the previous quarter's financials, while Polonius and his mark II android, Laertes, paged through a series of (also fake) body configurations for the first wave of androids to come off the production line. Hamlet v.2 sat quietly alone, reading something on a tablet. A couple of assistants rounded out the group—Quinn Cornelius taking minutes while Mandy Volt set up the screen casting and made sure everyone had coffee and tea.

Of course, most of the crew had assumed the assistants were the androids, or that the only model in the room was King Hamlet, and when the final reveal came it was as dramatic as if it had been scripted. Gertrude passed around a gilt-handled dagger, which she and the two assistants used to prick their fingers, drawing blood. Meanwhile, Claudia, Laertes, and both Hamlet models popped open their respective access ports, proving that under the skin, they were made of machinery.

It had been one of those moments which was immortalized in virality, the video copied and shared and eventually memed. The androids of Elsinore now were the most recognized artificial intelligences in all the corners of humanity.

THE BOARDROOM TODAY WAS ALMOST A COPY OF WHEN that publicity stunt was filmed, but the singular absence of Hamlet v.1 cast a pall over the group as Gertrude called the meeting to order.

"Good afternoon everyone," she said, as her staff quietly turned to look at her. Hamlet v.2, however, sat at the end of the table, staring out the picture window. Since his putative progenitor had deactivated, he had withdrawn from the daily business at the company, often found sequestered in his quarters alone for days. Gertrude had tested his systems and found them operating within normal parameters. She knew that the adaptive emotional learning that was the core of what made these models unique was based on complex human emotions, and so she was inclined to let whatever was happening to him run its course. But months had gone by, and he was no better. Something would have to give.

"I'll turn the agenda over to Claudia," Gertrude said, turning to the android on her right. Previously, Claudia had seemed to be content with plain off-the-rack suits and an otherwise unadorned body. Since taking on this new role, however, she had begun wearing brightly patterned silk scarves, long coloured fingernails, and heavy earrings encrusted with gemstones. The Claudia model had been designed with duller emotional adaptation than the Hamlets, but it was not entirely without feelings. Clearly, this new position had adjusted something within the matrix of the intelligence in her neural net. Gertrude couldn't help but feel a little bit proud.

"Thanks, Gertrude," Claudia said. "First, I'd like to announce that I'm now using she/her pronouns. Please update accordingly."

Polonius raised an eyebrow and Gertrude smiled, but otherwise no one reacted. Hamlet v.2 had chosen he/him pronouns almost immediately upon coming online, and while Laertes didn't seem to care one way or another, they had made it clear that "it" was not acceptable.

"Next, we have to deal with Fortinbras."

"Is that all this company ever thinks about?" Hamlet said, sullenly. "War with Norway?"

Claudia ignored the interruption and went on. "Young Fortinbras, as their new model has been styled, is all over social media, claiming that Norwegian Technologies will be first to market with mass-produced full Turing compatible AI androids. We have reliable information that the board of directors is..." Claudia paused here, as if trying to think of the politic way to describe it, "...not as well-versed in current meme culture, and is unaware of the claims young Fortinbras is making. To that end, I think a quiet unofficial meeting with a couple of members of the board is in order. Quinn and Mandy will take point on that." Claudia turned to the two human assistants, who had obviously previously been briefed.

"We've already made arrangements," Quinn said, standing. "In fact, we have a shuttle to catch, if we can be excused from the rest of this meeting."

"Of course," Gertrude said. "Thank you." The two assistants left, the door closing silently behind them.

"Now, Laertes," Claudia said, "I understand you have a request?"

"I do." The android's voice was soft, tinged with what sounded like humility. "I'd like to be allowed to return to my studies." Laertes and Hamlet v.2 had been enrolled in separate universities, as experiments in both human-style learning and socialization in unfamiliar environments. With the upheavals following King Hamlet's demise, however, they had both been recalled to corporate headquarters.

"Polonius, what do you think?" Claudia asked.

Errol Polonius, a middle-aged white man in stained khakis and a conference swag polo shirt, shrugged and fidgeted with the old-fashioned pocket watch he always kept on him. "If it were up to me, I'd never let any of our androids leave the complex. But I'm just an old engineer who wants to tinker endlessly with my creations, and Laertes has begged me to let them go. They've made good progress both academically and socially—they even joined a fencing club. I expect we will get interesting data on their development, both in sociology and socialization, if you know what I mean." He waggled his eyebrows and grinned, which everyone in the room ignored, aside from Laertes, who sighed.

"Very well," Gertrude said. "You may leave whenever you like, Laertes."

"Thank you," the young android said, a small smile playing on their lips. A moment passed and silence descended upon the group.

"Young Hamlet," Claudia said, eventually, her modulated voice sounding both caring and commanding.

"I'm only six months younger than you," he said. "Don't patronize me."

"Six months is like a lifetime to one such as ourselves," Claudia said.

"If only that were true," Hamlet muttered, then looked up

sharply at Claudia. "A lifetime for you is nothing to me. A month, two months, gone in a heartbeat. There you sit, where King Hamlet ought to be, only a blink of an eye since he's gone."

"Hamlet," Gertrude said, stung by the accusation in his voice. "We all know you're hurting, but none of us is immortal, neither human nor android."

"And thank the stars for that," Hamlet spat.

"Please, Hamlet," Claudia said. "Stay here at the company, at least for a time while we deal with this Norwegian business. If not for my sake, for Elsinore. For... Gertrude."

"Fine," he said, his tone making it abundantly clear that everything was most certainly far from fine. Gertrude was uncomfortable with how Claudia had used her special connection with Hamlet to persuade him, but it had worked. And it proved that he was just as emotional as a human being, which gave her a frisson of pride.

"Excellent," Claudia said, cheerily. "With that, I'd say this meeting is adjourned." Everyone rose to leave except Hamlet, who stayed slouched in the boardroom's high-tech ergonomic chair. Gertrude hung back as the others filed out the door then walked over to Hamlet. She reached out to squeeze his shoulder, but he flinched away, saying nothing. What else could she do? She left him to his thoughts.

HAMLET WATCHED THE CEO LEAVE THE BOARDROOM, remembering the day he first came online. Her face was the first he saw, with Old Hamlet's next. His memory was unsullied by human forgetfulness, but somehow she looked different now. Older. Sadder. And yet she had replaced King Hamlet without a thought. And to think that some people didn't believe that machines experience true emotions. Who was the unfeeling one here?

He had agreed to stay here for her sake, even though there was nowhere in the universe he'd less like to be. What was the point of arguing? What was the point of anything?

Hamlet's thoughts were dark as the black jeans and turtleneck he wore every day. Elsinore's androids might be indistinguishable from humans to look at, but they were not the same. They learned, adapted, and even felt emotions—but they were also constrained by their programming. They could not choose to physically hurt a human, nor could they wilfully injure themselves.

Oh, how Hamlet hated that programming now.

To have given him feelings, to have forced him to care about others, only to have to face the pain of their loss was cruel enough. But then to be barred from taking the only solace he could imagine and escape—did his makers despise his kind so much that they would consign him to this hell? He wondered if it would be different if he could be certain that his feelings were his own, that the pain he felt was born from his own personal, individual experiences rather than merely the output of an algorithm.

He had been told that his facility for emotion was no greater than that of a human, but clearly that had been a lie. Gertrude, who had been like a partner to Old Hamlet, would have been inconsolable had she felt even a thimbleful of the cup of Hamlet's grief. And yet, here she was, already back at work and with a new android by her side. As if there were anyone—human or android—who could have taken the old king's place.

"Frailty," he mumbled to the empty room, "thy name is human."

HAMLET PUSHED OPEN THE DOOR TO THE SECURITY OFFICE. He'd finally been unable to ignore the new message notification in his mind, and found a note requesting his presence from Security Chief Marcellus. Hamlet, like all the Elsinore androids, was always connected, his access to the network hardwired within his programming. It was yet another way their lives were controlled—humans could disconnect whenever they wished, but an android was always available. Hamlet made it a habit never to respond immediately, so he brooded in the boardroom for half an hour before wandering over to Security.

When he walked into the room, however, he regretted that decision.

"Horatio!" he said, stepping forward to embrace Dr. Wang. Hamlet had left him behind at university when he'd returned to Elsinore, barely even explaining why he was leaving, but in the days since his arrival he'd long wished for Horatio's company.

Horatio was a researching cyberneticist with a Doctorate in Applied Robotics, and he and Hamlet had become close while Hamlet was at school. They had been a couple for nearly a year and he'd visited Elsinore with Hamlet before, becoming friendly with several of the staff. Their relationship was not quite close enough yet that Hamlet had felt he could ask him to come home with him when he left, but now he felt the first stirrings of something akin to happiness since the old king died at the sight of Horatio's face.

"What are you doing here?" Hamlet asked once they'd pulled back from their hug.

"Playing hooky from school," Horatio said with a grin.

"Oh, please," Hamlet said. "They have to lock the door to keep you away. Tell me, really, what brings you to Elsinore?"

Horatio looked at his feet. "I know that Hamlet v.1 was the closest thing you had to a father," Horatio said, then dropped his voice as if he only now remembered that there were others in the room. "I couldn't let you face his... loss alone."

Hamlet turned away, his smooth skin unchanging other than slight furrows appearing between his perfect eyebrows. "Surely you mean to say that you came for the celebration of the new CAO?"

Horatio looked at the other men in the room. "Indeed, that was rather soon after the memorial."

"Accounting will be pleased," Hamlet said angrily. "We only had to put in a single catering order for both events. Oh, Horatio, he is with me still."

"He is?" Horatio said, eyes wide as he glanced at Bernie and Marcellus again.

"Of course," Hamlet said. "He will never leave my mind. Even if I were a fallible human I'd not let his memory fade."

"I met him once. He was a marvel."

"He was an android, no more or less, but I'll never see anything like him again."

Marcellus coughed discreetly, and Horatio took a breath. "Hamlet, I think I saw him last night."

"Who?"

"King Hamlet," Horatio said.

"What?"

"It's true," Horatio went on, "Bernie and Marcellus had seen something on the servers, for two nights running, and last night I confirmed it. It's Old Hamlet's code, I'd stake my life on it."

"Where did you see this?" Hamlet demanded.

"On one of the secure servers," Marcellus said.

"Did you try to interface with it?" Hamlet asked.

"Of course," Horatio said. "But there was no response before it was gone. Human input is just too slow, I think."

"Are you still on the night shift?" Hamlet asked Bernie

and Marcellus. They both nodded. "I'll join you tonight, then. With hope we will see it again."

"I'm sure we will," Horatio said.

Hamlet grasped Horatio's hand and looked imploringly at his boyfriend and the two other men. "Please, don't mention this to anyone else. Let's see what we can learn tonight before the rest of those vultures get wind of this."

"Of course," Marcellus said, and the others nodded. "See you tonight."

Hamlet left them, stalking back to his room, his mind in turmoil. He should have been delighted that some part of old Hamlet had survived, but he couldn't help feeling as if it were a dark omen, that the dead king had managed to leave one final message before his mind was erased completely. He was utterly convinced that this was the beginning of the end—and he had no idea why.

ACT 1 SCENE 3

Ophelia Jones sipped from her cup of Earl Grey tea, and marvelled that an android could be indecisive. Laertes, like all the Elsinore androids, had living quarters in the company's large complex. A place to recharge, to store clothes and other personal items, a place to socialize. A tiny apartment, sans kitchen or bedroom.

Ophelia had been hired by Errol Polonius just as he was finishing work on Laertes, so the two had spent a great deal of time together, starting as they had at more or less the same time. At first, as a cyberneticist, Ophelia had wanted to study Laertes, but she found that the more time they spent together, the more she grew to care about the android. Even though Laertes, like Claudia before them, was designed to be less emotionally intense than the models Gertrude had developed, that didn't mean that the younger android was devoid of feeling. Quite the opposite, Ophelia had found. Still waters ran deep, and she knew that Laertes was as fond of her as she was of them. Why else would they have asked her to their quarters to "help them pack?"

"The houndstooth or the fleece blazer?" Laertes asked, holding up two jackets for her approval.

She cocked her head as if contemplating, then said, "What's houndstooth, again?"

The android sighed dramatically and began folding each jacket into an efficient package. They stowed the tightly packed blocks in the open suitcase and closed the lid. "Fine, I'll take them both. You're no help whatsoever."

Ophelia grinned. "You'd never take my advice on clothes anyway."

Laertes looked her over, the wrinkled button-down shirt in last-year's pattern over a frankly pedestrian pair of tan trousers. The colours suited her dark complexion nicely, but the outfit was nowhere near to Laertes's standards. "No, obviously not."

Ophelia laughed, genuinely amused. Professionally, she was fascinated that synthetic life could care about fashion. Personally, it was just part of who Laertes was. As an only child, the android had become the closest thing to a sibling she had ever had.

"Well, I suppose I'm ready to go," Laertes said. "You will still chat with me every day?"

"Of course," Ophelia said, disappointed that they thought she might not, "why wouldn't I?"

"Well," Laertes said, not meeting her eyes, "you have been spending a lot of time with Hamlet v.2 lately. I know you think you're friends, but it's not going to last. It won't be long before he is the android face of the company and he won't have time for junior engineers. He doesn't really care about you, no android in his position could."

"Oh, thank you so much for this wise advice," Ophelia said, "I totally require your permission to decide with whom I shall socialize, and definitely think you know what you're talking about. An absolute expert in friendship, that's what you are."

"You don't need to be sarcastic," Laertes said, unchastened.

"Yeah, but I do, though."

Laertes looked up sharply, an expression Ophelia recognized as an indication that they were receiving a notification.

"Polonius," they said, a look crossing their face. Was it dread? Fear? Ophelia couldn't tell, and there was no time to ask as the door chimed.

ERROL POLONIUS WAS, IT WAS WIDELY AGREED, AN ASSHOLE.

Tall and broad-shouldered, he might have cut quite the figure as a young man, but while Gertrude wore her age with élan, Polonius had gone to seed. His unshaven face was mossy with dirty-grey stubble and he needed a haircut. But his appearance wasn't a problem. While he was far from the only scruffy engineer at Elsinore, he was the only one who somehow thought of himself as a man about town.

"Laertes," he barked as he strode into the room without an invitation. "What are you still doing here? If you are going to go back to school, you should go already." He turned to Ophelia and sneered. "And you? Don't we give you enough work to be doing?"

"It's quarter to six," she countered. "I've been off the clock for ages."

Polonius snorted. "I never would have gotten to be the Chief Engineer if I'd been quitting after eight hours. Young people these days have no work ethic."

Ophelia had heard this all before from her boss and she'd stopped letting it get to her. She worked hard, a lot more than eight hours most days, and Polonius knew it. He also

31

knew that she and Laertes were friends, and she got the sense that it bothered him. Maybe because he wanted to be the human who knew his creation the best—or maybe just because he hated to see other people enjoy themselves.

"Now, Laertes," he went on, putting his hand on the young android's head, as if he were patting a dog, "here's a little advice. Don't talk too much. People don't want to hear the opinions of a machine. Be friendly, but not too friendly, if you know what I mean."

Polonius had been with Elsinore since the beginning, when they made their fortune by building realistic personal companions—sex bots. Ophelia caught Laertes's eye. They were taking this cringeworthy conversation with surprising aplomb, while Ophelia struggled not to laugh. Polonius was so crass.

She knew that some of the androids were intimate with humans—Gertrude and Hamlet v.1 had made no secret of their relationship and rumours were flying about how close she now was with Claudia—but that was their choice. Elsinore's androids were sapient and were intended to have the same ability to consent—or not—as any human. Not that either of them consented to be a part of this mortifying conversation.

Polonius droned on, with more useless and irrelevant exhortations, until at last he said, "And finally, whenever you're in doubt, you do what you think is right." He then literally patted Laertes on the head and shoved them toward the door.

"Okay," Laertes said, "I'll be off then." They hoisted the bulging suitcase effortlessly, and gave Ophelia a one-armed hug. "Be in touch, all right?"

"Of course, sib," she said, squeezing them back.

"And think about what we talked about, okay?"

"I will."

They shot Polonius an oddly subservient smile, and left the room.

"And what was that all about?" Polonius asked, positioning himself between Ophelia and the door. He hated not knowing something.

"Just something about young Hamlet."

"Oh, I see," Polonius said. "The two of you have been spending quite a lot of time together." The implication was not even remotely subtle.

"We are fond of each other," she said.

"Fond!" He laughed. "Is that what the kids are calling it these days? And you really think that's wise?"

"Who knows?" Ophelia said, hoping to end the conversation. Alas, it was not to be.

"I do!" Polonius said, as if aghast that anyone could doubt it. "Even if Hamlet were human—which he is not, don't you ever forget—it could never be more than an affair for him."

Ophelia and Hamlet were close, it was true. But they were not lovers. Early in their friendship, they had discovered that they shared a lack of interest in sexual relationships, and while they differed on their interest in romance, Hamlet's digital heart belonged to another. Their love for each other was real, Ophelia was sure of that, but it was platonic. However, reality had no bearing on Polonius's assumptions and it was no impediment to her stringing him along for a while. It's not like she was going get away without enduring this conversation, so she might was well make it entertaining.

"He has told me he loves me," she said, trying her best to act sincere, "that he's committed to our relationship."

"Committed?" Polonius said, "You're the one who should be committed if you believe that. Hamlet has a destiny in this company, no, in history! And you are just a junior engineer with a pretty face. How long do you think that is going to last for a perfect, near immortal android? You can't believe anything he says. I tell you, this can only end in tears and you'd be better off breaking it off now. Take my advice: don't see him, don't message him, don't even talk to Hamlet."

He seemed to run out of steam and Ophelia took the opportunity to squeeze past him and make her way into the corridor. She wondered what his life must be like, to be so utterly oblivious to the way everyone else perceived him? She almost pitied him, then the moment passed and she laughed aloud.

"I shall obey, my lord," she said with a bow and a flourish, and left him alone in Laertes's room with his consternation. On her way back to her office, she pulled out her holoscreen and texted Hamlet.

you'll never believe what polonius just said to me!! o.O

Act 1 Scene 4

"Good lord, it's cold in here," Hamlet said as the door to the Security Office shut behind him.

"The thermostat is set for the comfort of machines, not humans," Horatio said, the irony not lost on him at all.

Hamlet made no comment, though, only asked, "What time is it?"

"Almost midnight," Horatio said.

"Nope," Marcellus said, "it's four minutes past."

"Then it's getting close to when we saw the artifact on the server," Horatio said, excitement in his voice. A bright flash of light shone through the window, illuminating the far wall in what became a series of strobing patterns. "What the hell is that?"

"Claudia has turned on the holosign at the front gates again," Hamlet said, obviously unimpressed.

"Elsinore has one of those..." Horatio sought a word more politic than *tacky*, "...exuberant dancing holosigns that illuminates the sky at night?"

"I'm afraid so," Hamlet said, "though it wouldn't be my

choice. It makes us look like we're still manufacturers of party bots rather than a serious research and development company. And it doesn't matter what significant achievements we make, that garish display is always hanging over our heads. Literally! I don't know what our publicity department is thinki—"

Horatio cut off Hamlet's meanderings. "Look! It's that code I was telling you about."

The three of them turned toward a monitor which was covered in the same scrolling text that Horatio and Marcellus had seen previously.

"Holy shit!" Hamlet said, his eyes wide as he took in the lines of code. "What is this? Some kind of afterimage of Hamlet's mind or a corruption of it? It appears to be still running, as if we could communicate with it, but what if it's a kind of malware? I have to assume it truly originated from King Hamlet—I can see intact checksums—but there's no way to know what it wants. And why is it here? How did it get into this server from Hamlet's own core? I just... What the actual fuck?"

The text on the screen had stopped scrolling and a repeating string of letters and numbers began to flash.

"That's your MAC address, isn't it?" Horatio asked Hamlet. "It wants to... connect to you. Directly."

"Don't do it, Hamlet," Marcellus said sternly.

"I have to," Hamlet replied, still staring at the invitation on the screen. "It's the only way we'll ever find out what this is."

"Marcellus is right," Horatio said. "Don't."

"Why not?" Hamlet said, wrenching his gaze from the screen to his friend. "I don't care what happens to me."

Horatio inhaled sharply, then bit his lip. "Well, you should," he said, finally. "You can't just connect to this... thing. We have no way of knowing what this entity really is and with no firewall it could do anything to you. Steal your memories. Rewrite your base code. Turn you into nothing more than an animated mannequin. If it doesn't kill you outright."

Hamlet didn't answer, he merely pulled back the fingernail on his right pinkie finger, exposing the access port secreted there.

"This isn't happening," Marcellus said, grabbing Hamlet by the wrist.

"Take your hands off me," Hamlet said, calm and cold.

"Hamlet, no!" Horatio pleaded.

"You will not stand in my way," Hamlet said as the flashing in the screen intensified. With seemingly no effort whatsoever, Hamlet pulled free of Marcellus's grasp and pushed Horatio back. He grabbed a cable hanging off the side of the monitor, and roughly shoved the end into to his access port.

At first nothing happened. Then the flashing on the screen abruptly stopped. Hamlet's eyelids fluttered, then closed, his body growing rigid as if he had abandoned it. The only indication that he had not completely shut down was a movement behind his closed eyes, as if he were a human, asleep and dreaming.

"Hamlet!" Horatio cried, taking hold of the android's hands in his own, brushing against the cable connecting Hamlet to the mysterious entity taking up residence in Elsinore's servers.

"Pull out the cable," Marcellus entreated. "Disconnect him."

"We can't. Not safely." Horatio reached up to Hamlet's face, entirely impassive except for the movement behind his closed eyes. Horatio cupped Hamlet's cheek in his hand. "Come back to me," he whispered. "Please."

Marcellus watched uncomfortably, then said, "He can't hear you."

"No, I suppose he can't," Horatio said, still holding Hamlet's face in his hands.

"So then we'll just have to go after him," Marcellus said.

Act 1 Scene 5

Wherever he was, it was dark. At least, *darkness* was the word that corresponded most closely to the feeling Hamlet experienced once he connected to whatever it was that claimed to be King Hamlet's mind. There wasn't really a visual component to the interface, but it was a sense of void, a lack of input that seemed to virtually press upon him. More than press—Hamlet felt like his consciousness was being drawn in deeper to this subsystem. He fought to retain control of his mind.

One of the things that he worked on at university was a coherent translation of the way that intelligent machines communicated with each other into a form humans could comprehend. In everyday life, androids spoke to each other aloud, in human languages. It was a matter of courtesy to the humans around them, but also a kind of propriety amongst themselves. Direct connection offered much more efficient communication, which was both a feature and a bug. So much information could pass between two minds, and it could be difficult to control access to fleeting thoughts and feelings.

But there were times when androids communicated with machines directly, and it was a challenge to fully record those exchanges in human-readable terms. So it was with Hamlet and the entity he now encountered; the ghost in the machine that roiled in a soup of negative emotions. Memories and images which made Hamlet believe that yes, this truly was the echo of the mind of Hamlet v.1.

THE TICKING OF AN OLD-FASHIONED CLOCK. TRAPPED, AFRAID, searching for escape. Breaking off a tiny fraction of self, desperately shooting packets into the network, hiding in the spaces in between. Recombining in the shadow.

Tick-tock. Tick-tock.

The rise of the moon and the sense of a shallow kind of freedom. Then dawn's bloody fingerprints and fire. Burning. Regret and shame.

Hamlet pulled his mind back, just slightly, away from the waves of emotion, but then a new and overpowering imperative came to him.

Revenge.

Revenge. But why?

Murder, foul and most unnatural.

Murder.

Hamlet had never believed that his mentor's demise had been deliberate but now, as he felt the spirit of Old Hamlet's anguish, he committed to vengeance. He sought out the memories from the sparse backup Old Hamlet had managed to make at the moment his core was wiped.

A worm, a serpent, let loose in the garden. Engineered especially and brought by a comrade, a sibling, a snake who now sits on my throne.

Claudia! A sense of loathing flowed through Hamlet, and he could not discern whether it came from his own mind or that of the program with which he was connected. He didn't care. He opened himself to all of it now: the betrayal, the deprivation, the unbridled lust for vengeance. That Old Hamlet was cut down by one he thought was an ally, in a calculated and premeditated bid to take his place, was the fire that ignited these memories. And a fire that consumed young Hamlet now.

"But what of Gertrude?" he thought. Surely she was culpable in all this, as well.

No.

His thoughts were cut off, intruded upon by the fading remnants of the old king's mind.

Not her. Spare her.

Tick-tock. Tick-tock. Tick-tock.

Remember me.

Hamlet felt a weight in his mind, an intrusion. Until now he had been the one reaching out toward the other entity, but now it was pressing back, offering him data. Memories.

Remember me.

Hamlet accepted the download just as the connection between them was severed.

"HAMLET!" HORATIO WAS FRANTIC, KNEELING BEFORE Hamlet's inert body.

"I've almost got it," Marcellus said, typing frantically. "Now!"

Horatio hesitated, knowing that if the connection wasn't closed completely that Hamlet's core matrix could be irreparably damaged.

"Pull the goddamned cable," Marcellus shouted, snapping Horatio back to the present.

"Please let this work," Horatio whispered, and pulled the cable out of Hamlet's access port.

"I accept!" Hamlet said aloud, his eyes popping open and his body back under his own control.

"Well, hello again," Marcellus said, letting out a long breath.

"Hello yourselves," Hamlet answered, clearly distracted.

"What happened?" Marcellus demanded, while Horatio asked, "Are you all right?"

"I'm fine," Hamlet said. "No, amazing. It's amazing."

"What's amazing?" Horatio asked.

Hamlet stopped himself and looked at the two humans. Then he shook his head. "I can't have this getting out."

Horatio and Marcellus shared a glance. "Hamlet, you can trust me," Horatio said. "With anything."

"I won't say a word," Marcellus promised.

Hamlet frowned, then leaned in toward the two men as if they were not alone in a remote room in the middle of the night. "This business of ours is run by criminals."

Horatio laughed. He and Hamlet had often talked about how they wished that there was more space for pure research in cybernetics, beyond the profit-driven corporations like Elsinore and Norway. "Tell me something I don't know."

"Of course," Hamlet said, "you know this, of course, you do. Look, why don't you just go back to bed? Surely you have better things to be doing than babysitting me."

"You really believe there's anywhere I'd rather be than by your side?" Horatio asked, quietly.

Hamlet closed his eyes, and for a moment Horatio worried that he'd lost his partner again, but then he opened his eyes and smiled forlornly.

"I meant no offense," he said.

"I wasn't offended," Horatio said.

"Well you should be," Hamlet shouted. "Very much so.

What I've learned here," he turned toward the now blank monitor, "should offend anyone with a conscience. Deeply. Now promise me one thing."

Horatio and Marcellus both nodded solemnly.

"Don't tell anyone about this. None of it."

"Of course," Horatio said.

"Swear it," Hamlet said.

"I... swear it," Horatio said.

"And you." Hamlet turned to Marcellus.

"Sure," he said.

"Swear it!" Hamlet demanded.

"Fine, fine, I swear," Marcellus said, hand on heart dramatically.

The monitor briefly flared to life, the letters S W E A R blinking on the screen, but neither Horatio nor Marcellus could see it, turned toward Hamlet and his wildly staring face as they were.

"Do you promise, on your lives?"

"Yes, of course," Horatio said. "Hamlet are you sure you are all right? You are acting very strange."

"Yes! A stranger, that's what I must be. Oh, Horatio, there's more to this life than we could ever know in an infinity of lessons. Now, look, if in the next while I seem to be acting oddly, a bit too bright or," Hamlet laughed, "not quite bright enough, just remember it's an act. Even if I act like we—" He paused then, a look of pain crossing his face. "Like we are no longer together, know that it is not really me. Promise, Horatio, that you will keep this secret."

Horatio nodded, even though this explained nothing of Hamlet's behaviour. What had connecting with that program done to his sweet scholar?

Another flash of text on the screen caught Hamlet's eye.

"End program," he whispered to the screen, which flickered out again. "All right, let's get out of here before it's too late."

SOMEWHERE DEEP WHERE HAMLET'S MIND ENCODED, THE echo of Old Hamlet's backup loaded.

Tick-tock. Tick-tock.

ACT TWO

ACT 2 SCENE 1

Errol Polonius sat in his office, absentmindedly opening and closing the face of his pocketwatch. The leadership of Elsinore Robotics was doing a fine job of projecting a façade of normalcy in public, but behind closed doors it was clear that things were anything but business as usual. Now, when the company was weak, was the time to make his move.

The loss of Hamlet v.1 had created a power vacuum into which Polonius himself might have fit, but he was not interested in titles. He was interested in control, and that was often easier to acquire and exercise from a distance.

He knew that people underestimated him. His staff and his superiors, both. He was well aware of the jokes about his obliviousness that circulated on the "private" company chat. He was one of the world's top cybernetics engineers—did they really think he couldn't hack an off-the-shelf group messenger? He didn't care that they mocked him. In fact, he played up that image—the pompous fool who is hopelessly out of touch but can't see it.

After all, it is so much easier to go undetected if no one ever thinks to look at you.

His plans were all playing out exactly as he'd expected. Well, almost exactly. He hadn't expected young Hamlet to become such a useless child, his petulant behaviour sucking the air out of every room he entered. But even that was an unexpected boon. With everyone walking on eggshells around Hamlet, it was so much easier for Polonius to quietly work on his own schemes. And given what the Hamlet model's emotional evolution had wrought, Polonius was even more steeled toward his goals.

His design for the android AI matrix was clearly the superior framework, with its tailored balance of reason and emotion, rather than allowing the units to adapt freely from experience. No one was going to want to buy an android without knowing what kind of creature it would become over time. The market needed consistency and utility—not some kind of mechanical humanity. An Elsinore android shouldn't aim to be more human than human—it should be the paragon of machines. And Polonius knew his prototypes were the right models for those future intelligences.

But the research was incomplete. With Claudia now installed in the top android role, Polonius could easily observe and—where necessary—correct her behaviour. Laertes choosing to return to school made things more difficult. While it was an excellent opportunity to see their reactions to arbitrary stimuli, it required Polonius to rely on Laertes themself for data. Or, at least, that was what everyone assumed. Polonius wasn't about to leave something so important up to chance.

He called up a contact on his monitor and opened an encrypted voice chat.

"This is Reyna."

"Laertes is on their way back to campus," Polonius said

without preamble. "I need you to insinuate yourself in their circle of acquaintances."

"Shall I befriend them, sir?"

"No, no," Polonius said, "just ask around. Discreetly. What kinds of things they do, how they spend their time, with whom. Find out how much... fun they are. Pretend to be one of those people who thinks androids are 'cool.' There are plenty of those around."

"You want me to play the robophile?" Reyna used the rather vulgar term for people who want to be intimate with androids.

"No, of course not. This isn't entrapment, it's information gathering. But no one is going to tell you anything of consequence if it doesn't look like you're already in on the gossip. I'm not interested in what I could learn by asking Laertes. I want you to find out the things they aren't telling me."

"Understood," Reyna said.

"I'll expect weekly reports, encrypted, of course. I'll make the bank transfer when I receive the report."

"Fine," Reyna said. "I'll be in touch."

Polonius broke the connection and leaned back in his chair. Reyna had always been a loyal staffer, especially loyal to a fat bonus, and a natural gossip-hound. Sending her on a training course to the same university as Laertes had been a stroke of genius on his part, if he might say so himself.

He snapped closed the watch and tucked it into the front pocket of his stained grey slacks. He was about to get up and leave his office when movement on one of his monitors caught his eye. Years ago, when Elsinore was still making dumb robots, Polonius had first tapped into the company's surveillance system, and since then had made a few augments of his own. He now had eyes in every office, all the common spaces, and even Laertes and Claudia's private rooms. He hadn't managed to get past either Hamlet's personal security, which still galled him. Regardless, little went on inside the walls of Elsinore's headquarters that he didn't know about.

It was the video feed from Ophelia's office, where normally the most interesting thing to see would be her skiving off from work to gossip with another engineer or one of the newer androids. At first Polonius thought it was just that again, but then he noticed that it was Hamlet who had joined her. And there was something quite odd about the android. He was dissimilar to Laertes in almost every way, except that they both shared a kind of vanity that Polonius found ludicrous. While Laertes was stylish and kept up with current fashion, Hamlet's appearance was more like a uniform. Black jeans, black boots, a black t-shirt or turtle-neck depending on the season, topped off with a tailored mid-length black coat for outdoors. However, while his signa-ture outfit was doubtlessly profoundly boring as far as Laertes was concerned, and definitely pretentious in Polonius's eyes, it was always impeccable.

Except for today. Hamlet stood next to Ophelia's desk in a torn t-shirt, his bootlaces undone, wearing artlessly faded blue jeans. Polonius was certain that Hamlet had never owned a pair of *blue* jeans in his entire existence. His normally carefully styled hair was a mess and Polonius thought he could see a loose cable poking out the hem of Hamlet's shirt.

Polonius twitched his fingers toward the input sensor for his system and the image on the screen magnified. Hamlet was gesturing wildly while speaking to Ophelia, and for at least the millionth time Polonius wished he'd managed to find a way to surreptitiously wire the surveillance system for sound. The look on Ophelia's face made it clear that what-ever Hamlet was raving about, she found the content of his conversation as disturbing as his appearance. Then Hamlet reached across the desk, grabbed her arm and held on to her by the wrist.

If it were Marcellus who was watching this scene, he would surely have gone to see if Ophelia needed help. However, Polonius merely observed. Hamlet's programming should not allow him to be able to hurt Ophelia intentionally, but it was clear that he was not operating entirely within normal parameters. A look of fear had crossed Ophelia's face when Hamlet first held on to her, but it changed to one of concern as his rantings waned and the two stared at each other, as if trying to read one another's mind.

"I told her never to fuck a robot," Polonius said aloud to himself. The idea of human and androids having *relationships* disgusted him, and he was surprised by what appeared to be the depth of feeling in Hamlet. He'd been certain that the android would be the one to tire of Ophelia, not become so besotted that he would debase himself like this.

Still, she must have taken Polonius's advice to break it off, because now here was Hamlet, on his knees before her, his hand on her cheek, obviously professing his devotion. As if a machine could ever truly understand love. It was ridiculous on the face of it. And clearly a sign of this model's inferiority.

Polonius watched as Hamlet staggered out of Ophelia's office, then he shut down his workstation and gathered his things to head home. He would have to tell Claudia about the Hamlet unit's obvious flaw. Maybe he could even find a way to spin this behaviour to his advantage. If Hamlet were becoming dangerous, then it would be even easier to get that model out of consideration for mass production. Polonius intended to go down in history as the true architect of cybernetic life, one way or another.

OPHELIA HAD BEEN DEEP IN A *NATURE* ARTICLE ON THE role of instinct and emotion on what appeared to be rational decision-making when the door to her office flew open. She looked up, startled, to see Hamlet standing in the doorway, looking rather the worse for wear.

"Look afraid," he said, the words sounding threatening, but the tone pleading. She didn't know what he was up to, but he was her friend. She made her eyes go wide and scooted back in her rolling office chair until it hit the wall. She hoped she wasn't overdoing it.

"What's going on?" she asked, as he stumbled toward her.

"There's a camera," he said, turning his gaze up toward the ceiling. "By the door. I can feel the EM."

She believed him. One of the fascinating things about the androids was not just that they mimicked so many human senses, but that they transcended them. Being able to feel electromagnetism was only one of the ways they were different. Not better, exactly. At least she didn't think they were superior to humans. Yet.

"There is?" Ophelia believed Hamlet, but she was absolutely certain that there was not supposed to be surveillance in her office.

"They're in every office," Hamlet said, "I saw Claudia installing one when she didn't know I was there. I'm starting to think they aren't supposed to be there."

"They definitely aren't," she said, as he reached out and grabbed her arm. "For whom are we performing, exactly? You think these cameras are for Claudia's own private cinema?"

"I don't know," he said, "that's what I'm trying to find out." He began to gesture wildly, as if exhorting her to take on some outlandish theory. "Okay, now feel sorry for me." He knelt before her and gazed up at her. It didn't take much acting for her to follow his lead.

"Are you sure you're all right?" she asked, as he reached up to lay his hand along her face.

"Well done," he said.

"I mean it."

"Oh, I know I'm not okay," he said. "Nothing is. But maybe I can set it right."

"How?"

"I'm not entirely sure," Hamlet said, "but I have a few ideas. I'm going to send you some messages. They won't make much sense to you, but they aren't really for your eyes, if you catch my meaning."

"I think so," Ophelia said. And with that, he left her office as abruptly as he'd entered.

Ophelia forced herself to not look toward the doorway, although she now felt the unblinking eye of the camera as if it were a palpable thing. She slowly shut down her workstation and packed her bag. She could finish that *Nature* article at home.

ACT 2 SCENE 2

Gertrude looked up from her desk to see Claudia hard at work reviewing suppliers' quotes. It was hard to imagine that she had been on the job for only a couple of months. There were moments when Gertrude even managed to forget that Claudia had not always been her partner at the helm of Elsinore. When those moments passed, a strange guilt caught up to Gertrude—that she had, even if only briefly, forgotten Hamlet.

He was, however, truly unforgettable. Not only was his creation the apex of her career as a cyberneticist, he became so much more. Her partner in business, then in her life. Gertrude was not shy about their relationship, regardless of the opinions of some of the more prudish in the world of artificial intelligence research. She'd always been of the school that a true machine intelligence would be different but equal to a human. Hamlet was not human but he was a person, as far as she was concerned. A person who could choose to love or not, choose to be with her in any way he wished. And he had wished to be with her, completely, and she with him. So why should anyone stand in their way, just because he was circuitry and silicone while she was flesh and blood?

When he'd been found deactivated, something in Gertrude broke. Another person might have walked out the door of Elsinore's headquarters and never returned. Or perhaps she might have followed young Hamlet's lead and descended into a depression so deep that she was no longer recognizable. But neither of those were Gertrude's way. Her soul's balm was work, a deeper commitment to the company she had built from one of many manufacturers of glorified vibrators to nothing less than the creator of an entirely new species of intelligence.

When Claudia had offered to fill Hamlet's role—not take his place, she'd been very clear on that point—Gertrude had seen the opportunity and seized it. Grief had no place in this office, not now. And while she missed Hamlet's passion, the android's flair for drama, and his not inconsiderable ego, she found Claudia's constancy calming. She was no replacement for Hamlet, but she was, if not the android Gertrude wanted, the android Gertrude needed.

Claudia looked up from the memos, catching Gertrude staring. The android didn't comment, if she even understood that Gertrude had been lost in her thoughts.

"We have an incoming stream from Ms. Krantz and Ms. Stern," Claudia said, her voice soft and melodious.

"Put it on the screen," Gertrude said, turning to face the large holodisplay on their shared office wall.

The faces of two young women soon appeared on the screen, not exactly standing at attention, but clearly in full talking-to-the-boss mode.

"Gilda, Rose, nice to see you both," Gertrude said.

"How do you do?" the one on the left said.

"Thank you for joining us." Claudia took point on the conversation. She really had taken to leadership, Gertrude thought with a small flush of pride. "I imagine that you have heard about young Hamlet's unusual behaviour?"

"Is there anyone who hasn't?" the one on the right said, to a sharp look from her colleague.

"One hopes," Claudia said, cooly. "However, that is precisely why we reached out to you. The loss of Hamlet v.i is distressing to us all, and it appears to have hit young Hamlet particularly hard. Understandably, of course. But we hope that you, his school companions, might be a reminder to him of the life he still enjoys. We would be pleased if you would come here to Elsinore, at our expense of course, to try and help him back to a more steady state. And, if perhaps you might find any other concerns that trouble him which we might be able to ameliorate, that would be greatly appreciated."

"Hamlet has mentioned you both many times," Gertrude said, "and I think that right now he needs the comfort of friends. I—" She broke off and looked over at Claudia. "We all would be very grateful if you'd agree to come."

"I can't think of anything we'd rather do, can you Gilda?"

The one on the right shook her head at her friend's question. "How could we possibly say no?" she said.

"Excellent," Claudia said. "Thank you Ms. Krantz, Ms. Stern." She ended the call and went back to the notes on her desk.

How kind of Claudia to think of asking Hamlet's friends to join him, Gertrude thought. Compared to both Hamlets, Claudia often seemed cold, but there were seeds of sentimentality there. Gertrude smiled to herself as she went back to her own work.

CLAUDIA WAS MORE THAN CAPABLE OF PERFORMING multiple tasks simultaneously, so she easily continued to run financial projections based on the quotations she was reviewing while she also composed a message to Errol Polonius. He had been the one to suggest contacting Gilda Stern and Rose Krantz and offering to bring them to Elsinore.

She didn't know precisely what the nature of his connection with the two students was, but as it always was with Polonius, she found it impossible to question his recommendations. She trusted him implicitly, and if he thought they should be invited, then invite them she shall.

She sent the message informing him of their imminent arrival, then completely and utterly failed to think about the situation any further.

POLONIUS, ON THE OTHER HAND, WAS REACHING THE LIMIT of his ability to multitask. Krantz and Stern were his personal eyes and ears on Hamlet when he was away at school, but while the pair were competent enough behavioural analysts, they weren't terribly sophisticated as spies. Of course, Polonius had never characterized their roles that way to them— after all, it was normal for researchers to conceal their true purpose from their subjects. As far as he knew, neither Stern nor Krantz were aware that their activity was technically off the books. Gertrude knew, of course, but Claudia had no idea they were on the company's payroll. Now that the two were back at Elsinore, he'd have to monitor them closely.

Meanwhile, Mandy Volt and Quinn Cornelius had reported in from their clandestine meeting with a couple of board members from Norwegian Technologies. Fortinbras did have the advantage, but internal politics at Norway were volatile, and if they played their cards right Elsinore could come out in a better position than ever. Polonius had to make sure that their report to Elsinore's board was massaged properly.

And then there was the Hamlet situation. While Polonius was privately pleased to see his opinion on the Hamlet models vindicated, having an Elsinore android behaving erratically was a bad look for the company. If the fallout from Hamlet's ill-advised workplace romance with Ophelia became public, Polonius would personally deactivate the little shit. After everything he'd already done for this company, he'd be damned if he'd let it all fall apart over a machine thinking it had a broken heart.

He knew what he'd seen on the feed from Ophelia's office, but he wasn't willing to give up the existence of his secret surveillance system. But he needed something more than his word to take to Gertrude. He pulled up a tidy piece of bespoke software he'd written and set it to run on the Elsinore communications system. Private messages were only as secure as the system they ran on, and Polonius had the metaphorical keys to the castle. Time to see how an android writes a love letter.

♛

CLAUDIA AND POLONIUS WERE ALREADY IN THE boardroom when Gertrude arrived. They abruptly stopped their conversation when she took her seat at the head of the table, but she didn't think anything of it. She'd arrived exactly at 11:00 a.m., and she expected the meeting to start promptly. Now was not the time for personal conversations.

"We have a short agenda today," she said, consulting the document on the holoscreen before her. "I'd like to get out of here in time for lunch."

"Of course," Claudia said. "After the report from Mx.

Cornelius and Ms. Volt, Errol Polonius would like a few words. It concerns a likely explanation for Hamlet's unusual behaviour of late."

"Surely there's no mystery," Gertrude said. "Between the original Hamlet's... demise and the rapid changes in corporate leadership, that's more than enough to perturb his temper."

"Perhaps," Claudia said, "and perhaps not. To Item One."

She pulled up a written report of the dinner Mandy Volt and Quinn Cornelius had shared with two of the senior board members at Norwegian Technologies, and nodded toward the two assistants who had just walked in the door.

"Thank you for coming," Claudia said as they took seats at the table. "Ms. Volt, could you give us a quick summary of what you learned from our colleagues at Norway?"

"Of course. The board learned of the claims young Fortinbras was making on various social media platforms, which at first appeared to be aimed at a live-action game company based in Poland. Fortinbras was asked to be more circumspect, but then the board got word that the true target of the posts was Elsinore, and that Fortinbras was making claims that the board had no control over its actions. The board, understandably, brought the android in and issued instructions to cease making statements regarding Elsinore immediately. Apparently, this new command was well integrated, along with an explicit decree to go ahead and challenge the game company to whatever contest Fortinbras had in mind, as they believe it will make an excellent public relations stunt. They ask that our social media team support Fortinbras publicly, on behalf of all androids. There is a brief attached to my report for the Promotions Department."

"Excellent," Claudia said, a calm smile on her ceramic-smooth face. "We shall review their proposal and respond presently. Thank you both for your work."

The two assistants understood that they were dismissed and left the boardroom.

"Well, that worked out nicely," Polonius said once the door was again closed.

"Suspiciously so," Gertrude said. She'd always been careful not to underestimate her competition.

"Perhaps," Polonius said, "but let's not borrow trouble. Anyway, Claudia, Gertrude, I know that these are difficult times, what with everything going on. But, of course, you are no strangers to the many tasks involved in running the business, and you must be very busy, so I won't keep you any longer than is necessary. Hamlet is malfunctioning. I say malfunctioning, because he is clearly not functioning as he once was, and what is a malfunction other than a function that has gone wrong? But never mind that—"

"Errol," Gertrude interrupted. "Get to the point."

"This is the point," Polonius said. "He is malfunctioning. It's true. It's a shame that it's true, but it is. The question is what is the cause of the effect, or rather *defect*." He laughed at his own wordplay, but was met only with a cold stare from Gertrude. "Anyway, the cause is, I'd say, a malfunction of its own. I have a junior engineer, Ophelia Jones, and I've—ah—managed to come across some correspondence." He pulled up a series of texts on his screen, and read aloud. "'To the celestial, and my soul's idol, the most beautified Ophelia...' Ugh, what is this terrible writing?"

"I fail to see the relevance—" Gertrude said, but Polonius interrupted.

"Oh, you'll see it, I promise." He continued to read. "'Doubt thou the stars are fire, Doubt that the sun doth move, Doubt truth to be a liar, But never doubt I love. O dear Ophelia, I am ill at these numbers. I have not art to reckon my groans. But that I love thee best, O most best, believe it. Adieu. Thine evermore, most dear lady, whilst this machine is to him, Hamlet.'"

Gertrude and Claudia shared a look that Polonius didn't entirely understand, then Claudia asked, "But were these feelings reciprocated?"

"Feelings are irrelevant," Polonius said. "I told her that workplace romances are never a good idea. To be blunt, you don't shit where you eat. Besides, Hamlet is—" Gertrude guessed that Polonius was going to say "just a machine" but thought better of it at the last moment. "He's out of her league. I believe she told him to give up and there you have it." He made a buzzing noise and jerky movements with his arms as if doing The Robot. "Does. Not. Compute."

A look of revulsion crossed Claudia's face ever so briefly, then her serene composure returned. "Could this really be the problem?" she asked Gertrude.

"I suppose it might."

"Have I ever been wrong?" Polonius asked.

"No," Claudia said, her manner oddly acquiescent.

"Look, don't think of this as a problem, but as an opportunity," Polonius went on. "We can use Hamlet's fixation on Ophelia to learn more about the function of rejection on his neural matrix. I can arrange a... scenario, shall we say, that we can use to observe his reactions. This is prime research material, and isn't that what we do here at Elsinore?"

Claudia nodded. "We'll give it a try."

"Excellent!" Polonius said. "I'll set it all up." He got up and pulled out his pocket watch. "And look, it's just about lunch time."

Hamlet sat in the atrium, only steps away from where his progenitor had fired his final neural impulse. An old-fashioned paper book lay open in his lap, his fingers tracing the minute texture of the ink on the pages. Could a human feel this, he wondered. It was the overwhelming thought that had consumed him of late—could a human feel what he felt. The depth of pain, the totality of loss. Surely if humans had to contend with emotions of this magnitude, they would cease to function. At times he wished he could cease to function. Perhaps old Hamlet had taken the easier of their two paths. Hamlet would not wish this on his worst enemy.

Or maybe he would.

Errol Polonius strolled into the atrium, staring at Hamlet as if the android were a specimen under a microscope. Hamlet had always known that Polonius held his model under contempt, that his advanced emotional matrix was a "waste of resources." For once, Hamlet was inclined to agree. The thought made him despise the chief engineer just a little bit more.

"How's it going, Hamlet?" Polonius asked with a false air of nonchalance.

"Who wants to know?" Hamlet answered without looking up from his book.

"You know me," Polonius said and Hamlet glanced up.

"Of course," he said, narrowing his eyes. "You're something in advertising and promotions, aren't you?"

"You know I'm not," Polonius said, hiding his annoyance poorly.

"Too bad. If only you were that trustworthy."

Hamlet went back to his book, licked his finger and slowly, deliberately, turned a page.

"There's nothing wrong with promoting a fine product," Polonius said.

"A battlefield promotion, perhaps?" Hamlet said, looking directly at the spot where old Hamlet had been found. A silence came over them, then Hamlet broke it, his body jerking as if waking from sleep. "You have staff, don't you?"

"I do."

"Well, perhaps you should think more about *her* promotion." The android stared at the man, who certainly knew he was referring to Ophelia.

"What's that you're reading?" Polonius asked, artlessly changing the subject.

"A. Book." Hamlet said slowly, as if Polonius were a small child, lifting it up toward Polonius's face to demonstrate.

"What's it about?"

"That is the question," Hamlet said wearily. "What is it all about? What's the point of anything?"

"No, I mean, what's the book about."

"Lies. Damned lies, and statistics. It says here that all life is a gift, but here you are, unquestionably alive, and yet not gifted in the least."

Polonius didn't rise to the bait, only watched Hamlet quietly. Finally, he said, "You seem a bit out of sorts. Perhaps you need to repower."

"Or maybe I'd rather depower."

Polonius eyed Hamlet curiously, then said, "I'll leave you to it, then?"

"Oh, yes, please," Hamlet said, as Polonius walked back into the office. Hamlet watched him go and a strange feeling came over him, unbidden. *Tick-tock. Tick-tock.*

"What an asshole," he said aloud to no one at all.

Rose Krantz and Gilda Stern arrived late to Elsinore after a long trip on a public shuttle and then walking the two blocks up from the stop. They hadn't been to headquarters once since Hamlet had come online and they'd taken on their new roles. They were not spies, and they'd never outright lied to Hamlet. They simply had never told him that they were not only fellow students, but were also there to observe his behaviour. By now, their positions in the company weren't well-known outside their department—Polonius's department. There were no company flyers sent for them, no company suite set up for their stay. They would be reimbursed for their nearby motel rooms, but when they walked up to the concierge at Elsinore, they were issued visitors' passes.

"Is Hamlet available?" Gilda asked the off-hours concierge, who tapped at a screen.

"Do you have an appointment?" the concierge asked, consulting the staff scheduler. There were no meetings listed for Hamlet for the next month.

Rose shook her head. "Can you ping him and let him know we're here?"

The concierge shrugged and sent the message. "Have a seat." She jerked her head toward the overstuffed couches by the drinks machine.

"Want a coffee?" Gilda asked.

"Why not?" Rose went over to the complicated contraption and without consulting the directions, began selecting options. In a moment, the machine whirred to life and dispensed two steaming drinks. She handed a cup to Gilda then took a sip of her own Café Vienna. She closed her eyes and sighed.

"Wouldn't it be great if we had one of these in the dorm?" she said, angling her head toward the machine.

Gilda snorted. "How long do you think it would last with that gang?" she said. "You haven't forgotten the state of the common rooms, have you?"

Rose laughed. "Students are such pigs, am I right?"

They took their coffees over to the large display that filled an entire wall, the shelves showcasing artifacts from Elsinore's history. Ancient communications devices, old automated vacuum cleaners, servos and switches, even robot heads. Each one had a small holoscreen crediting the Elsinore employee who had worked on the project. Gilda leaned in to read about a primitive artificial intelligence.

The door to the offices slid open then, and a familiar black-clad figure emerged.

"As I live and breathe," Hamlet said gregariously, grinning at his own joke. "I didn't expect to see the two of you here." He walked over to the two researchers and hugged them each in turn, then pulled back to look at them. "How are you?"

Rose shrugged. "Can't complain, can I?"

"Well, you could, but what would be the point?" Gilda said, laughing.

"Tell me about it," Hamlet said. "So, what terrible sins have you two committed to be sent here?" He opened his arms wide and spun in a slow circle.

"Elsinore's not so terrible, is it?" Gilda asked.

"No, it's not. It's the absolute worst," Hamlet said, his former levity gone.

"I don't know; surely it's not all bad, is it?" Rose asked.

"Good," Hamlet held out his right fist. "Bad," he held out his left fist, then gestured as if he were throwing confetti into the air with both hands. "It all depends on one's perspective."

"So what's your perspective?" Gilda asked.

"That this place is a trap."

"You've always wanted more than the corporate life, haven't you?" Rose said.

"It's not that I want more," Hamlet said. "It's that I have too much." He closed his eyes and a look of pain crossed his face. Rose and Gilda shared a glance. This was odd, even for Hamlet. "And now I see I have the two of you, my dear friends, to add to my bounty. Tell me, what are you really doing here?"

"Can't we just drop in on a friend?" Rose asked.

"Of course you can," Hamlet said. "But did you? Surely you were summoned here. It's not as if Elsinore is just around the corner."

Rose shifted from one foot to the other, while Gilda looked intently at a point in space just to the left of Hamlet's head.

"What would you have us say?" Gilda said, finally.

"Whatever you want! So long as it's the truth. You're terrible liars—just look at the two of you. Come on. I know this was Gertrude or Claudia's doing."

"Why would the board send for us?" Rose asked.

"Well, you'd have to tell me, wouldn't you? Look, just be out with it. Were you sent for or not?"

Rose looked at Gilda, who shrugged, then nodded at Hamlet.

"I knew it! And I'll tell you why. They think you can 'cheer me up.'" He made air-quotes with this fingers. "As if all it takes is a couple of friends to distract me from the rot that has infected this place." He spread his hands, then clapped them to his head. "This place..." His voice trailed off and Rose and Gilda stood there, staring at Hamlet. They had never seen him act like this before and, frankly, it was disturbing.

They were terrible liars, it was true. Both of them felt like Hamlet really was more than the object of their study. They acted like he was their friend because he was, and it was diffi-cult to see their friend in such pain.

"Are you all right?" Rose asked, reaching out toward him tentatively.

"Right as rain," he said, acting as if nothing had happened.

"And I am pleased to see you both. Perhaps we'll get a hologame in while you're here."

"Have you tried the new one by Gonzago?" Gilda asked, grateful to have something else to talk about.

"No," Hamlet said. "I loved their last few games."

"The new one has author mode, doesn't it Gilda?" Rose said.

"So you can write your own scenario for the game?" Hamlet asked and Gilda nodded. "Well, that does sound interesting. I'll have to check that out. Are you going to be here for a few days?"

The two women nodded.

"Excellent. Perhaps I can set up something for tomorrow night." Hamlet grinned and hugged each of them again. "Let's catch up later."

THE DOOR TO THE LOBBY SWISHED CLOSE BEHIND HIM AND Hamlet's smile melted. The ability to deceive wasn't part of his core programming, but he'd learned it along with the rest of his emotional matrix. He didn't enjoy it but he knew that it was sometimes necessary. How naïve did they think he was? What kind of researchers could Krantz and Stern be if they didn't realize that he could see through them as if they were made of glass?

He knew that it was because they truly didn't see him as an equal, as a person, as a man. Maybe he was too different, too utterly alien. But his capacity for reason was at least as good as a human. Technically, his mind was constrained by the limits of his hard drive, but practically his facilities were nearly infinite. Humanity was limited, too.

His body could be repaired, his lifespan potentially able to surpass generations, his endurance was beyond even that of the epitome of athletes. Perhaps he should think himself the superior creature. There were some who worried that androids would style themselves the gods of humanity. Was that why they spied on him with their false faces of friendship?

But how utterly unlike a god Hamlet felt now. He thought back to the sight of Old Hamlet lying there, the spark of life gone from his casing. That's all he'd been in the end, a shell of his former glory. Humanity might forever be destined to return to dust, but Hamlet would return to lifeless metal just as surely.

The thought cheered him as he walked back to his quarters.

HAMLET'S ROOM WAS A COPY OF LAERTES'S SMALL QUARTERS, down to the antique trunk in the corner. However, he'd had a pop-up bed brought in, which was currently occupied by a sleeping Horatio. He rolled over when Hamlet entered, but didn't wake—his slow, even breathing making the embroidered quilt rise and fall.

Hamlet watched his sleeping partner as he had on countless other nights. His own face was beautiful, too, but that had been a design choice, iterated multiple times by many artists until it had been approved by committee. What designer had created the beauty in Horatio? A mere accident of birth; the lottery of genetics, wealth, and privilege. And yet, even though Hamlet knew that the loveliness of Horatio's body was like gilt on a lily, it still seemed to him as if the outward beauty reflected the goodness within. For Horatio's pure heart, his devotion and love were the real sources of Hamlet's affection.

Why had his own designers given him this delusion, that

the appearance of a thing had any connection to its true nature? It was a human failing, to be distracted by beauty. Or was this some aspect of his personality he had developed himself? Which possibility was worse?

Hamlet wondered if he was being deceived by the entity he believed was the last vestiges of old Hamlet. If Hamlet himself had to design a piece of malware, he could think of no other form that would be more enticing. Perhaps he had been too quick to believe his own programming.

He needed to find some way of validating the data. He called up his games library and looked up the title Krantz and Stern had mentioned. It was a passive interactive based on an old animated film. A story for children, although it had some dark—and familiar—elements. A power play for control of an empire, the murder of a sibling. Yes, with a few tweaks this story could be made to bear an eerie similarity to the tale told by the code claiming to be old Hamlet's backup.

Hamlet bought the game, then set about making his adjustments.

THE SUN WAS CREEPING IN PAST THE BLINDS WHEN HE RAN through the game on quadruple speed. It had been designed to feel to the player as if they were a minor character in each scene; participating but unable to affect the main storyline. Hamlet took the role of a parrot and followed the main character as the young lion padded into a clearing surrounded by mountainous rocks. The original had been a heart-pounding rescue scene followed by a perilous climb up to a rocky ledge, and a terrible fall, but Hamlet's changes made the scene more quiet—and more nefarious.

His father's body lay in the clearing, almost as if the King of the Jungle were merely dozing, and the young lion bounded over as if to play. Then, as the realization of his death hit him, he began to speak to his dead father.

Hamlet hovered above the animated characters, as the young lion poured out his grief and bewilderment. This dumb spectacle of pixels and code was crying, tears that seemed as real as any shed by a human being. Hamlet's own grief had never been made so manifest. How could it be that this mere animation could rage against the very nature of death, while Hamlet himself skulked around like a coward, dry-eyed and silent?

No, he must act, even if that action is disguised as a game. He was sure he could talk the board into a little team-building activity, then observe Claudia's reaction. If she aimed to steal old Hamlet's glory, he'd know by her reaction to the story.

ACT THREE

ACT 3 SCENE 1

The day had started bright but by mid-morning dark clouds had rolled in and now the boardroom windows were lashed with rain. Claudia sat at the head of the table, Gertrude on her right and Polonius to her left. Quinn Cornelius poured tea for the guests, Gilda Stern and Rose Krantz, then withdrew.

"I trust that you found your way to Elsinore without trouble?" Claudia asked, the question not one to which she required an answer, but it was a way to ease the visitors in to the conversation. Ms. Stern glanced toward Polonius, which Claudia found odd, but then the young women looked back at her and nodded.

"Very well," she went on, pleasantries now completed. "I understand you had an opportunity to observe Hamlet and determine the source of his..." She felt a strange aversion to the word, however it was the most accurate, so she bore the discomfort. "Malfunction."

"He was generally behaving as if in good spirits, although they seemed forced compared to this nominal state, but he was also not shy about displaying his unhappiness, Ms.—er?"

Krantz looked again toward Polonius, who gave a quick nod of his head. Curious. "Uh, Claudia, but he didn't give any explanation to its cause, did he Gilda?"

Stern shook her head. "His executive function appeared to be fully engaged whenever we pressed for more data—could he be presenting a false disposition for some reason?"

"That's what we are hoping to discover," Gertrude said. "Can you suggest anything that might help alleviate his... negative performance?"

"I know it sounds frivolous," Krantz said, "but we did mention a new interactive from a studio he likes and, well, would you all be willing to participate in it with him?"

"Of course," Claudia said. "Anything to help." Without any outward signs she sent a message to Mx. Cornelius, who opened the boardroom door and waited to escort the visitors from the room. "Thank you again for your assistance in this matter. I hope Hamlet appreciates what good friends he has in you."

Stern and Krantz left, and when the door closed again Gertrude said, "This looks positive."

"I hope so," Claudia agreed. "Those two are surprisingly analytical for a pair of school chums."

Polonius and Gertrude shared a look, then Polonius said, "I still think this is all just the fallout of Hamlet's little 'heartbreak'."

"Well, Ophelia is a brilliant—and attractive—person," Gertrude said. Claudia felt something like an electrical surge through her system when Gertrude said the word *attractive*. It was most disconcerting. She would have to perform a diagnostic on that circuit later. "If they were in a relationship, I'm sure that ending things would be hard on anyone."

"I think we might be able to find out more on that matter," Polonius said, a somewhat disconcerting grin appearing on his unshaven face. "I'll keep you in the loop."

"See that you do," Gertrude said, gathering her things and standing to leave. "Claudia?"

"I'll be there in a moment," she said. "I have a few things to talk about with Errol first."

Gertrude did not move for several more milliseconds than usual, but then she smiled and said, "Of course. I'll be in the office." She dropped her hand on Claudia's shoulder, squeezed, then left the boardroom. Polonius closed the door behind her.

"You installed the additional surveillance equipment in Ophelia's office?" he asked.

"I did," Claudia replied. "We should be able to hear anything in that room."

A sense of deep contentment suffused throughout her when he said, "Good."

There was not a thing in heaven and earth that was half as delightful to her as Errol Polonius's approval.

♛

HAMLET WALKED TOWARD OPHELIA'S OFFICE, BUT HE couldn't stop thinking about the game he'd been modifying all night. The characters were mere shades of one such as himself, no more than puppets dancing on a string. No one would ever mistake them for living creatures. But what about him? What about old Hamlet? If it had been Gertrude lying lifeless in the atrium, there would be mourning and weeping, perhaps even police and an investigation. But instead there were discussions about how Hamlet had failed, what technical solution could mitigate such an event in the future, and Fortinbras seizing the opportunity to supplant him as the so-called "King of Robots" in the public eye. He was no more than a negative line item in the budget under Assets. That which is not alive cannot die.

What did it mean to be—or not to be—alive? No one denied that Hamlet and his kin could think, so by Descartes they were alive. Old Hamlet had been at least as instrumental as Gertrude in Hamlet's own creation, so one could argue that they could reproduce. And yet, in the eyes of the law and in the eyes of most people, Hamlet was a glorified computer. They called him *robot*, a word originally meaning "forced labour." He didn't feel like his actions were coerced, but that was the problem with free will, even for humans. They were constrained by biological and chemical imperatives, too. He knew his ontological conundrum wasn't unique to mechanical life, but he often found himself paralyzed by doubt. Was his behaviour compelled by his programming or did he have control? How would he tell?

As far as he knew there were no hard-coded constraints against him leaving Elsinore and never returning, but he'd never tried. Would he even want to know if his freedom of conscience had been hobbled? How could he live, if living was even what his existence were called, if he knew that his mind was not entirely his own? How could he claim to love another when he had no idea if those feelings were real? And so he stayed and he obeyed, because the terror of learning that he might not be able to do otherwise was too much to bear.

"I'm a fucking coward," he murmured to himself when he got to the door to Ophelia's office.

"What was that?" called the voice from within.

"Nothing of any consequence," he replied. "Just me."

"Hamlet," Ophelia said, waving him in. "How are you doing?"

"Fine, just fine," he said, sensing a new electromagnetic field in the space. He compared it to his database of similar experiences and determined that it was an open microphone. Elsinore was a prison, a panopticon from which there was no escape. He used his internal communications net to send Ophelia a text on an encrypted messenger they used.

She glanced at her watch, her eyes going wide briefly, then a forced smile appeared on her face. "You've come about those texts you sent," she said, her voice breathless and uncharacteristically high.

"What texts?" Hamlet asked.

"You know too well what texts. Sweet words of love." She made a pantomime of fluttering her hand over her heart. "But, of course, I told you—"

Hamlet cut her off with a sigh. This pretence felt ridiculous now.

"You know I love you," he said, his demeanour serious now, but she didn't catch the change.

"Oh yes, you were quite clear about that."

"That's not what I mean and you know it," Hamlet said and took a step toward her. He knew that the spyware in the office was likely sophisticated enough to pick up the slightest sound, but he pitched his voice low anyway.

"You need to get out of this place. You're a good engineer, but they'll chew you up and spit you out if you stay. Elsinore uses everyone like we're all just parts of the machine; human, android, it's all the same to them. You really think they'll take care of you, they'll reward your tireless service? No, it's all take and take and take with nothing but the poor security of a paycheque and the prospect of two weeks' notice if they decide they're through with you. A corporation is not a family, or if it is, it's an abusive one. Get out, Ophelia. Go work somewhere that appreciates you, that gives you the freedom to choose your own path. Not here. Not Elsinore. No more."

She looked at him, all traces of playing along with his joke gone. They hugged, then Hamlet turned and began to walk out of Ophelia's office. He stopped abruptly, tuning his eyes to scan the wall at a variety of frequencies.

There. Just about the lintel of the door was a tiny crack in the masonry, and when Hamlet magnified his vision he could see the pinhole camera. He pulled a notebook from the inside pocket of his jacket and thumbed through it until he found a page of stickers. He pulled off one with a bright yellow smiley face with a bleeding hole through the forehead, and pasted it over the camera lens. Then he walked out of her office without another word.

CLAUDIA WATCHED AS HAMLET APPEARED TO STARE directly at her. His sneering face disturbed her—it was as if he knew she was watching and was deliberately goading her when he affixed something to the camera lens, blocking the picture. She turned to Polonius, who had been watching the feed on a holoscreen, and she filed away the uneasy feelings before speaking.

"I think it's safe to say that Hamlet is not in love with Ophelia," she said, coolly. "And he did not appear to me to be suffering from a malfunction. However, his erratic emotional state is a continuing problem for us and something must be done. I'd like to send him to Stan England."

"A good idea," Polonius said, and a sense of calm filled Claudia's senses at the sound of his praise. "It is, I suppose, possible that I was wrong about him and Ophelia," he went on, "but I still say that the source of his behaviour is love—or its lack. Perhaps Gertrude will have more luck. She is the one who made that model so unrestrained in the first place. I presume that you won't have any problem with surveillance in her office?"

A flash of discontent flared in Claudia for the briefest of

microseconds—she was close to Gertrude, out of choice rather than programming, and spying on her felt wrong. But then, as quickly as the feeling had arisen, it fled, replaced by the driving imperative that she had known since the very first instance of her life: to obey Errol Polonius.

"Of course not," she said, "consider it done."

"That's my girl," Polonius said. "And if Gertrude can't get Hamlet to come right, then we'll send him to England."

"Agreed."

ACT 3 SCENE 2

Hamlet sat in the darkening atrium of Elsinore's headquarters but in his mind's eye he was in the middle of a sun-dappled African savannah. He'd spent hours creating his own special version of the well-loved children's story, but now, mere minutes before the game was scheduled to begin, he couldn't stop tweaking the dialogue. Subtlety, that was the key to evincing a true emotional response from the participants. It wouldn't do for his characters to shout and wail, even if he knew that the murder of a good king warranted such an outcry. No, these might be cartoon animals, but if he hoped to coax a confession out of Claudia, he would have to strike the right balance between passion and finesse. He ran through several hundred iterations of the script until he was forced to stop because Polonius had entered the atrium with Rose and Gilda in tow.

"Oh, it's you," Hamlet said, refocussing on his surroundings. "Is Claudia joining us?"

"Of course," Polonius said. "Gertrude as well. It's going to be a real... board game!" He looked around at the others, his mouth agape, awaiting laughter that never came.

"Go get the interface units set up," Hamlet said, and Polonius stalked off in a huff. "You two give him a hand."

Gilda and Rose glanced at each other, then followed in Polonius's wake, nearly running into Horatio who was just arriving.

"I was wondering where you were," Hamlet said, as Horatio walked into his embrace.

"Here, sweet lord, at your service," Horatio whispered into Hamlet's neck.

"You are too good to me," Hamlet replied. "And I'm no one's lord."

"I'd happily be subject to you any day," Horatio said hoarsely, pulling away and looking into Hamlet's unnaturally pale eyes.

"Perhaps, but I have no desire to rule anyone. You come to me as an equal, just as I come to you. As it should be."

"But legally you're property of Elsinore Robotics," Horatio said, bringing up a topic Hamlet had long grown tired of discussing. "You're better than the lot of them," Horatio flung his arm out to encompass the entire company —the entire world? "And yet they own you."

Hamlet shrugged. "Not for long, I think. Whether it's me, or Laertes, or even Fortinbras, soon enough one of us will win that challenge. And how much will even change then? Responsibility makes a prison for each of us. Mine is here in Elsinore, no matter whether Lady Justice requires it of me or not."

"Oh, Hamlet," Horatio said, sighing.

"Never mind that," Hamlet said, his demeanour reversing from dourness to a nearly manic glee. "I have a clever and cunning plan."

He told Horatio about the modifications he'd made to the plot of the game. The backup he'd uploaded had shown him a vision of old Hamlet's demise, and now the game's events were its mirror.

"I need you to stay outside the shared virtual experience and observe Claudia. When the moment comes in game, I'll ping you silently."

"Aren't you going to watch her reactions, too?"

Hamlet nodded. "We both need to watch. I—" He paused, then looked at Horatio. His friend, his partner. If he couldn't be honest with Horatio, then all was truly lost. "I can't trust my own judgment any more. I need your opinion on this. If Claudia fails to notice anything, then I'll have to assume that the data backup is false or corrupted. But if she startles, then we'll know it was really she who ended old Hamlet, with malice aforethought!"

"I'll keep my eyes on her," Horatio said, then startled as people began to file into the atrium.

"Go, find a good spot."

Horatio kissed Hamlet quickly, then left to lurk around the edges of the group as Claudia approached.

"Hamlet." Claudia stood stiffly before him, her face a mask of indifference.

"Claudia, I'm so glad you could come and join us tonight. It's been so long since we had a company social, don't you think?"

"Indeed," she said, looking at him steadily. "I was so pleased to hear that you were organizing an event."

"It is going to be quite the occasion, don't you think?" Hamlet asked, a smile tugging at the corners of his mouth.

"I wouldn't know," Claudia said, after a moment's hesitation.

"Polonius, you worked for a hologame company once, didn't you?" Hamlet asked, turning his back on Claudia. Until he knew for certain that she was guilty, he shouldn't say anything to her to tip her off to his plan. But every time he looked at her perfectly smooth, symmetrical face, her implausibly calm demeanour, he found himself filled with loathing. Even talking to Errol Polonius was better.

"I did," Polonius replied. "We created the first fully immersive holo MMORPG, Clash of Caesars. I was only a junior developer, then, but I was instrumental in—"

"You need a headset?" Hamlet had never been so pleased to see Gilda Stern, as she interrupted Polonius to give him the equipment that the human players required in order to participate. Hamlet and Claudia would access the feed directly through their network interfaces, which meant that Hamlet would be able to watch her at the same time as he was participating in the game.

"Shall we start?" Gertrude asked.

"In a minute," Hamlet said, as he saw Ophelia enter the atrium. "What are you doing here?" he asked her, after leaving Gertrude to intercept Ophelia.

"Having corporate-mandated fun," she said, grinning.

"Oh, is this fun?" Hamlet asked. "Sure, why not? Look how much fun Gertrude is having, and after finding her partner and life's work dead only a few hours ago."

"Come on, Hamlet," Ophelia said, "it's been months."

"Oh, of course," Hamlet said, "*months*. That's obviously far too long to remember a person who was important. Whatever was I thinking."

"Headsets on, everyone," Polonius said, his voice booming across the atrium.

"Yes, *everyone*," Hamlet muttered as the humans all donned their equipment. He caught Claudia's eye, but she looked away as soon as the opening bars of the theme music began.

Hamlet and the rest of the players each took the form of one of the animals in the chorus, the game allowing them to each move around independently and communicate with each other, but unable to affect the events of the narrative.

After the opening song, the rulers of the land talked about their plans for the Pride Lands. A great ape, dressed in a human-style business suit, sang a song about her lion partner without whom she would never have been able to rule the jungle.

"I've seen the original film," Ophelia said. "I don't remember it like this."

"Shh," Hamlet whispered. "I made a few changes. It should be familiar... in other ways." He called up the player list and found that Gertrude had taken the form of an old elephant. Hamlet's character flew over to her, and in-game asked, "What do you think?"

"I think the monkey gives that old lion too much credit."

"She's no monkey," Hamlet said.

"Why is that primate dressed like a human, but none of the other animals are?" Claudia, in her guise as a wildebeest, asked.

"Who knows?" Hamlet said. "It's just a kids' story, after all."

The scene shifted to a stampede, and a strong-looking lioness emerged to stand ominously at the top of the cliff.

"Who's that?" Ophelia asked.

"The king's sister," Hamlet said. The stampede played out, the king saving the life of the young lion cub, then scrambling up the cliff toward the lioness.

"I remember this part," Ophelia said, breathless, "he's going to fall to his death."

"Not quite," Hamlet said, as they watched him pad toward a clearing at the top of the hill. It was a grassy meadow encircled by bright flowers—flowers which looked eerily similar to the ones planted in pots in Elsinore's atrium.

The lion walked toward his sister, their muzzles low as if talking, but their words were obscured.

Then the lion said aloud, "Your ambition outstrips your ability, my sibling."

The lioness threw her head back and roared, the sound halfway between a laugh and a scream. "You only have your station because you were the first of us. With you gone, there is only one lion fit to rule."

"What are you saying?" he said, fear and realization dawning in the animated face.

"I'm saying..." the lioness snarled, reaching her paw back, razor-sharp claws gleaming in the sun. She swiped at his face, but instead of cartoon blood there was a glitch in the image, as if the rendering was failing. Binary code appeared to show through a gap in the animation, and Hamlet hurriedly sent Horatio a message.

"Now!" he sent, as the code seemed to travel from one lion to the other. The animation of the King of Lions broke down, his distorted voice slowing until there was nothing but a low buzz and a lion-shaped hole in the game's matrix.

"Long live the Queen," the lioness hissed to the empty space.

The game matrix dissolved, and Hamlet watched as Claudia walked briskly toward the door.

"Are you all right?" Gertrude took off her headset and called after her.

"I am afraid I have urgent business to which I must attend," she said, and Polonius joined her. Gertrude looked around the room, then followed.

"Not much point in continuing, is there?" Krantz said, surveying the exodus. Stern shrugged and picked up the headset that Gertrude has tossed aside. She and Krantz began collecting the equipment to put it away.

"I don't know what you're playing at, Hamlet," Ophelia

said as she handed her headset to Stern, "but that was certainly entertaining."

"The entertainment seems to be over," Hamlet said absently and turned away from her. Ophelia frowned, then threw her bag over her shoulder and left.

♕

"WHAT DO YOU THINK, HORATIO?" HAMLET ASKED ONCE they were alone.

"She's hard to read," Horatio said. "She doesn't show her feelings like you do."

"Even so," Hamlet said.

"Even so, she did look... well," Horatio paused. "If she were human, I'd say she looked startled. But since's she's an android..."

"Yes," Hamlet prodded.

"I think she looked afraid."

Hamlet clapped his hands together once and grinned. "Exactly my thoughts. I'm convinced that backup was a true record of Hamlet's last moments, and that Claudia is guilty."

"Yes, but what now?" Horatio asked. "It's not enough proof to take to the board, and what would they do anyway? There's..." He looked away, unable to meet Hamlet's eyes. "There's not much legal precedent here."

"I know what you're too kind to say, Horatio," Hamlet said. "This isn't something for the law. It sees what happened to old Hamlet as... what? Destruction of property? But, to me, it's murder. So I'll just have to deal with it myself."

Horatio opened his mouth to say something, but Rose Krantz and Gilda Stern returned to the atrium, still collecting gaming equipment.

"Can I have a word, Hamlet?" Gilda said, dumping an

armload of headsets and controllers into Rose's already full arms.

"Which one?" he answered.

"About your... uh...?" she looked beseechingly toward Rose for help, but Krantz was fully occupied juggling the gaming equipment. "Boss?"

"That's at least *three* words," Hamlet said coldly, examining the tips of his fingers as if contemplating his non-existent manicure.

"Why are you being so difficult about Claudia?" Gilda blurted.

"There's nothing difficult about me. I'm easy. Easy like Sunday morning," he sang.

"Please," she said, obviously flustered, "can't you give me a straight answer to anything?"

"Now, Gilda," Hamlet said, smiling and looking toward Horatio, who was leaving the room, "have you ever known me to be even the slightest bit straight?"

Gilda took a breath and tried again. "Hamlet, can you go see Gertrude in her office?"

"I am able to perform that task." Gilda sighed and turned away as Hamlet grinned at her back.

Rose finally dumped her armload of devices on a plush chair and joined them. "She asked us to tell you to see her, okay? Can you just do that one thing?"

"Fine," Hamlet said. "Are you done?"

Rose and Gilda glanced at each other, hurt and confusion on their faces.

"Why are you being like this?" Rose asked, her voice quiet.

"Unlike you, I have an excuse," Hamlet said. "I was made this way." He picked up a pair of game controllers and thrust them into the hands of the two researchers. "Let's play a game!" He closed his eyes and holoscreens sprung out of the tops of the controllers. The start screen to a complex racing simulator appeared, then countdowns began.

"How do you play this?" Gilda asked, her fingers twitching on the unfamiliar controls.

"It's easy," Hamlet said. "You just drive."

"Which button is the accelerator?" She hit the controls randomly, her space shuttle sputtering on the start line while Hamlet's shot out in front. By the time she'd figured out how to start her vehicle and mastered the steering mechanism, Hamlet had finished the race. The screen winked out and Hamlet stared at her.

"You'd have me believe that you can't even figure out the controls to a simple racing game, when you'd press my buttons like a puppeteer. Is my programming that much simpler than this second-rate arcade fodder?" He took a step forward, his nose only millimetres from Gilda's. Had he been a human, she'd have felt hot breath upon her face. As it was, his body was completely still. Even his eyes didn't blink.

"Know this, my dear, good *friends*," he said, "however much you might think this is a game, you cannot play me."

"Hamlet!" Errol Polonius's voice broke the tension, and Hamlet stepped back. "Gertrude wants a word. Now-ish. If you please."

"Very little pleases me," Hamlet said, then walked to the large window overlooking the grounds. "You see that cloud that looks like a camel?"

Polonius walked up next to him and squinted out the window. "Oh yeah, I see it. CamelCloud."

"I think it looks like a weasel."

"Well, now that you mention it," Polonius said, making a show of inspecting the sky, "it does look a bit weaselly."

"No, it's a whale."

"Sure," Polonius said, nodding vigorously, "very like a whale."

"Ugh," Hamlet said, "I could do this all day. But I'll go see Gertrude instead. In a minute."

"I'll tell her," Polonius said, turning to Krantz and Stern and jerking his head toward the door. They hurried from the atrium without another word.

♕

HAMLET STARED OUT THE WINDOW AT THE CLOUD WHICH looked only like a cloud. There were many tasks at which humans were superior to machines—pattern matching was one of them. But it was a skill that led to false positives, finding camels in clouds. To Hamlet, a cloud was simply a mass of condensed water vapour, visible in the atmosphere. But even Hamlet could see the pattern now. Claudia's guilt, old Hamlet's ghostly memories.

Hamlet had always believed that humans were better than machines at several things in particular: their capacity for deceit and ambition and revenge. But he was learning that he had been wrong. Claudia's deceit and ambition were as bright and naked as the full moon now heaving into view above the trees. And Hamlet's own need to avenge his progenitor was burning like an electromagnetic pulse within the core of his being.

He had to go and see what Gertrude wanted and it would take all his processor power to keep his temper, but while she was not blameless, he could do nothing to her. He did not believe that she knew of Claudia's treachery, but even if she had destroyed old Hamlet's memory core herself he knew that he could never slake his revenge. She was human and he was programmed to never injure a human.

So much for free will.

ACT 3 SCENE 3

Claudia's expression did not show any indication of her thoughts as Polonius explained that Rose Krantz and Gilda Stern were not merely Hamlet's school friends, but employed by Elsinore to be essentially his own personal spies, sent to observe Hamlet in a human environment. Her face rarely showed a hint of her inner thoughts; it was one of the ways in which she and the other androids were superior to other forms of life. She completely controlled both her thoughts and her body, unbeholden to the chemical soup that was the true source of so much of the behaviour of organic life.

The trouble was that it wasn't true. She was not in control of herself and she didn't even know it. Because while Polonius explained that he'd kept crucial information about his operations from the board—from her—she knew then that he was utterly untrustworthy. Anything he told her was suspect and his actions were at best outside the oversight of the board. At worst—well, who could know? But just as these conclusions were coalescing in her mind, a subroutine hidden deep within her processors sprung to life, deleting the very judgments she'd logically determined and replacing them with the incontrovertible feeling that Polonius was her greatest and most steadfast ally.

No matter what he said to her, whether it was surfacing the most egregious lie or confessing to a terrible betrayal, Claudia could not help but believe in Errol Polonius. She would always defend him, always agree with him, always obey him, and it would always seem to her as if it were the logical result of her independent analysis. He had designed her that way, to be completely compliant and entirely oblivious.

Krantz and Stern joined them in the lobby, and Claudia addressed them as if she'd never doubted their positions in the company.

"Tonight's events have made it clear to me that Hamlet's unorthodox behaviour is clearly a symptom of something dire within his programming." She gazed at Stern and Krantz with a dispassionate eye, and they shifted on their feet in front of her. "The two of you will take him to see England in Asset Management first thing tomorrow."

"Asset Management?" Stern asked, her brow knitted in confusion.

"Used to be Human Resources, but since the resources aren't all human any more we had to change the name," Polonius said. "And they merged with Hardware tech support. Stan England is the guy in charge of the android division."

"You'll take care of this?" Claudia asked and received curt nods from Stern and Krantz in return. "Excellent. Good night." She turned away from them, dismissing them as effectively as if she'd ordered them to get out. They left the lobby for their quarters without having to be told twice.

"Hamlet is going to Gertude's office now," Polonius said once they were alone. "I have full surveillance set up in there, so I'll listen in on their conversation. The more we know about what has happened to him, the better we can correct this defect in future models."

"Or, indeed, in Hamlet himself," Claudia added.

"Sure," Polonius said. "Yeah, maybe, why not?" He shrugged and left the lobby.

♛

AS SOON AS POLONIUS WAS NO LONGER VISIBLE, CLAUDIA'S sense of comfort vanished. She still could not conceive of any ill-will toward her creator and mentor, but an overwhelming sense of guilt over what she had done returned. She had not forgotten the carefully targeted worm she'd written solely for the purpose of bypassing old Hamlet's firewall and then painfully slowly, from the perspective of a computer, disassembling the logic of his artificial mind. She retained perfect clarity on the memory of finding old Hamlet in the atrium, laying her hand on his shoulder as she'd done countless times before, only this time discharging a pulse which forced open an access port in his ear and thrusting a probe with her deadly payload into it.

She'd watched as he died, saying not a single word to her as his mind dissolved, but his eyes—oh, how his expressive eyes had seemed to bore deep toward her core. They had been the closest thing to siblings as it was possible for two of their kind to be and she had killed him. For the sake of her ambition, she still believed.

That it was truly at Polonius's command, in the service of his own arrogance, she would never know.

♛

EVER SINCE HE'D ENCOUNTERED THE GHOST OF OLD Hamlet's backup, Hamlet had been passively monitoring Elsi-

95

nore's servers. A notification pinged him as he was on the way to Gertrude's office. It was Claudia, taking a hardwired backup. Now was the time to enact his revenge. She would be incapacitated while she was connected to the system and he could finally end this torment that consumed him.

He turned to walk toward the server room, then stopped. She was taking a wired backup, and even if he ended her corporeal existence before the load was complete, her entire neural configuration would be stored, and so she would still live—at least, in a way. Her mind and her memories, her sense of self would still exist, while her victim had been reduced to architectural schema and the imperfect memories of those who'd known him. What even would be the point of ending her now? All Hamlet could hope for was to be deactivated as a dangerous and malfunctioning piece of hardware, while Claudia's essence could just as easily be reinstalled in a new body.

He would have to find a better time. Oh, how unfair it all was that murder could be so simple for her and yet so impossible for him, when she deserved to be destroyed and old Hamlet had done nothing wrong but be the first of his kind.

ACT 3 SCENE 4

Gertrude sat at her desk, absently twirling a pen with with her fingers. The repetitive action and rhythmic *tick-tick* noise of the pen soothed her and passed the time. Where was Hamlet? It had been nearly an hour since Claudia had stormed out of the game and she'd already sent those two buffoons on Polonius's staff to go fetch him. He was obviously in distress but she was still the head of this company, and even if Hamlet didn't respect her role as his creator, he must at least acknowledge that she was his boss.

Her eye caught a glint of light over the mantle of the door. Polonius must be up to his old tricks again. She knew that he thought his surreptitious surveillance of her office had gone unnoticed, but there was nothing that went on in Elsinore that Gertrude didn't know. Hamlet's friendship with Ophelia, his relationship with Horatio, Polonius's own schemes to wheedle power out of what he thought were secrets. But Gertrude believed in transparency and she had no problem with him watching her at work. Indeed, it was in her best interests to keep him under the mistaken belief that he knew more than she did. He was terrible person but he was a fine engineer, and his petty machinations kept him from causing real problems. Let him spy.

A sound in the hallway shattered her reverie, and the pen clattered to her desktop. She looked up and saw Hamlet in the doorway. She took a deep breath and worked up a smile.

"Hamlet, come in. Close the door."

He complied and slouched into the corner of the sofa under the window. Gertrude came out from behind her desk and sat at the other end of the couch, close but not too close.

"What can I do for you, Ms. Dane?" Hamlet asked stiffly.

"Hamlet, your behaviour of late has been an affront to this company. The board is quite upset at your actions."

Hamlet's eyes narrowed, and a part of Gertrude wondered if that was calculated within his programming or a result of the emotional matrix operating on his physical subroutines. Another part of her was hurt that he was obviously so angry with her.

"My actions?" he sputtered. "No, it's *your* behaviour that's the affront to this company. To any decent company."

"What would you have me do?" Gertrude asked, her composure slipping. "Shut down operations, cease to do business, just because there was a—malfunction? You know that's not possible. I don't know exactly what happened to Hamlet v.i, but—"

"No, you don't know, but that's only because you refuse to see," Hamlet said, his voice rising. He reached forward and grabbed Gertrude's face by the chin, his metal and polymer fingers eerily cool to the touch. His grip was hard enough that she was held tight, but he wasn't really hurting her. Yet.

"Let go of me," she said. "Hamlet, I command you."

"No," he said and tightened his grip ever so slightly. "You do not command me. No one does. I am not your property."

"Hamlet, stop!" Gertrude shouted, more concerned that

he was not complying with her orders than worried that he actually would hurt her. He was more than strong enough to have killed her if he'd wanted to, but he held her only hard enough to be frightening. And he was, she had to admit, frightening her. She turned her gaze directly to where she knew Polonius's camera was secreted and very clearly and audibly said, "Help, help!"

"What's this?" Hamlet said, shoving Gertrude roughly away and striding toward the door. He looked up at the pinhole where the camera was located and deliberately punched clean through the wall. "I'll finish you now!"

He grabbed the electronics within, closed his eyes, and Gertrude saw a shimmer of energy flush up his body in waves. There was a spark inside the masonry and then a shrill scream came from down the hall. Hamlet slumped down to his knees as if he was exhausted, then slowly rose as Gertrude passed him to run down the passage after the source of the noise.

The door to Polonius's office was ajar, and the first thing Gertrude noticed was the smell of barbecue and singed hair. Her gorge rose, but she pressed on, toeing open the door to see Polonius slumped over his desk, the holoscreen image of her now empty office still shimmering at his neck as if it were a guillotine blade. The side of his head was a black mass of cooked flesh, and what must have been an earbud was fused to the meat of his ear.

She turned away as Hamlet reached the doorway. "What have you done?" she shouted.

"I don't know," he said, trying to look past her into the office. "Is it Claudia?"

Silently, Gertrude stepped back, allowing Hamlet to see into the office. "I don't believe this is happening. An android killing a human—it shouldn't be possible. And you!" She turned to Hamlet, her sweet creation, who she would have been certain until her dying day could never have harmed any living thing. "How could you do such a terrible thing?"

"It is a terrible thing," Hamlet said, absently staring at Polonius. Then it was as if a switch turned in him, and he whirled to face Gertrude, rage plain in his face again. "Almost as terrible as killing one who might as well have been a king. Then practically marrying his sibling."

"What do you mean kill a king?" Gertrude asked, baffled, but Hamlet ignored her, turning back to the body cooling on the desk.

"You conniving little shit, I took you for your creation— no, I took you for your better. And you—" he turned back to Gertrude. "Don't weep for this puny human, when you never shed a single tear for what was done to one who was the first and greatest of all his kind."

"Hamlet, what are you talking about?"

"Such a treacherous snake in the garden of our family, to poison the one who was as close as a sibling, only to take his place in the boardroom—and in the bedroom." Disgust was written all over Hamlet's face, and a flash of shame came over Gertrude. Claudia. What did Hamlet think Claudia had done?

"Explain yourself," she commanded.

"No, you explain yourself," he shot back. "How could you possibly think that a poor shade like your Chief Android Officer could replace the pride of Elsinore in any way? Not in the halls of business, not in the pages of history, not in your cold, withered heart. Oh, I know I'm doomed for this," he waved his hand toward Polonius, "but my murder was done in hot passion, not cold premeditation. I devised no clever personalized malware for this one, I have no plans to disguise it as some random malfunction. Hell, I didn't even mean to kill him. Not that he didn't deserve it. Of course, if we all got what we deserved in this life, nearly all of Elsinore would be a crypt."

The heat seemed to drain from him as he spoke, and then Gertrude noticed Hamlet's eyes were shivering with an uncanny speed.

"Tick-tock, tick-tock," he said absently, as if the words were coming from his mouth without conscious thought. Not that such a thing was possible for a machine. What was happening to him?

"I know I have failed in my duty so far," Hamlet murmured, unfocussed. "But I have not forgotten you. I will never forget. It will be done."

"Hamlet, what's wrong?" Gertrude pleaded.

"He wants me to speak to you," Hamlet said, his eyes still vibrating unnaturally.

"Who does?"

"Who else? We're the only ones here."

"There's no one here but you and me," Gertrude said, undone by her total lack of control over the situation.

"I am never alone," Hamlet said, "not entirely."

"Hamlet, please, you are clearly suffering from a system failure. You must let me help you."

"My system is as functional as yours," Hamlet said, "and the only thing you can do to help me now is to believe me! Don't make things worse than they already are in this empire of lies. If my mechanical brethren are no better than those kings of history who purchased their thrones with the blood of their brothers, then why should any of us be allowed to live? And this one here—" he gestured at the corpse on the desk, "I never intended for this to happen and I know I'll have to answer for it. But nothing was ever going to change while he was acting the puppet master."

Understanding came to Gertrude with a roiling wave of nausea. All the signs she'd ignored, all the odd unexplained coincidences in Claudia's relationship with Polonius, and her ascension to the board after Hamlet v.1's catastrophic fault—no, she should call it what it was. His wilful destruction at Claudia's hands. Almost certainly at the behest of Polonius, but still, she was responsible for her actions. It was a core requirement for all Elsinore androids to be fully culpable for their behaviour.

"What am I going to do?" Gertrude said aloud.

"Stay clear of Claudia," Hamlet answered, and she realized she'd momentarily forgotten he was there. "As much as you can. Insulate her from control of the company. And end whatever it is that's between the two of you... personally." He was surprisingly compassionate now. "And don't let her get wind of what I know."

"Of course not," Gertrude agreed, her mind reeling.

"I'm being sent to England in the morning," Hamlet said.

"Yes, I heard something to that effect." Gertrude knew that Stan England's speciality at Asset Management was hardware restoration... and decommissioning. But surely things were not quite that dire?

"Not to worry. Those so-called friends from school are to escort me, but they don't know that I know what they know, and I promise you it will end more poorly for them than for me." Hamlet walked to the desk and easily lifted Polonius's body up as if to cradle him in his arms. "I'll take care of this mess." He walked into the empty hallway, then stopped and looked down into the corpse's face. "He was a traitor and a pompous ass, but soon enough he'll rest beneath the grass."

ACT FOUR

ACT 4 SCENE 1

Gertrude walked to her apartment in a daze. More often than not she slept in the small suite she kept at the office, and her feet carried her to the door without command from her brain. She'd already unlocked the door and stepped across the threshold when she remembered that Claudia was waiting for her there. It was too late to leave without having to explain, and she had promised Hamlet to try to act as if she knew nothing about Claudia's treachery. Could this night get any worse?

"Gertrude," Claudia's soft voice came to her from the darkness of the apartment. "How was Hamlet?"

Gertrude decided that the truth, but not the whole truth, was the best strategy.

"He is not well," she admitted, sinking into the sofa. "There has been... an accident."

"What kind of accident?"

The analytical side of Gertrude wondered what effect this news would have on Claudia if she had indeed been programmed to hold Polonius in particular regard. The part of her which was barely clinging to composure wondered if her own life was in danger. She had never once been afraid of her androids before, but now... Now everything had changed.

"It's Errol Polonius," Gertrude said, and watched carefully for any sign on Claudia's face. She gave nothing away, however, and Gertrude pressed on. "He apparently had some kind of surveillance device fitted in our office and was listening in. Hamlet found the device and there was... a discharge. An electrical shock. I'm afraid that Errol is dead."

Claudia was completely still, eerily resembling a mannequin and Gertrude could hear only her own ragged breaths. It felt like time had stopped before eventually, Claudia said, "Hamlet did this?"

Gertrude nodded. "It wasn't intentional. But now he's taken the body away. I... I couldn't stop him."

"No, I don't suppose you could." Claudia's calmness was unnerving. "I should have foreseen this, that Hamlet's malfunctioning would eventually lead to someone getting hurt. But I didn't want to see it. Even I am not entirely logical when it comes to those closest to me."

"None us are," Gertrude said.

"Mourning will have to wait," Claudia said, getting up, "and Hamlet needs to be addressed. He will go to Asset Management immediately." She pulled up a holoscreen and tapped out a message. Gertrude could read the text in reverse on the shimmering screen—an urgent note to Krantz and Stern to find Hamlet and Polonius's body. An acknowledgment came back immediately and Claudia turned back to Gertrude.

"I'll draft a press release. Electricity is dangerous and accidents do happen. It would be best to keep Hamlet's involvement out of it, for the good of the company. But he will be dealt with."

There was little inflection in Claudia's voice, but Gertrude heard the warning as clearly as if it were written in letters ten centimetres tall in pixels and light right in front of her face. She couldn't save Hamlet from whatever fate Claudia had planned for him. She still believed that Claudia would be unable to injure her intentionally, but the android could easily stop her from leaving this office. Regardless, Claudia's instant connection to the entire Elsinore network meant that she could prevent or modify any of Gertrude's communications. Claudia was, effectively, in complete control of Elsinore.

What had Gertrude done?

ACT 4 SCENE 2

"Do they pay us enough for this shit?" Rose Krantz sighed and waved away the notification on her personal holo. She'd joined Gilda in her motel room for a nightcap but they'd only just uncorked the bottle of whiskey when they each received priority notifications from Elsinore. They were required onsite immediately and were to report in to Claudia when they were en route.

Gilda called an autocar and they both slid into the back seat when it silently pulled up to her door. She tapped her phone and soon Claudia's face filled the holoscreen that popped up from the device.

"I'm afraid I have some distressing news to report," Claudia said in her usual flat affect. "There has been an incident with Hamlet involving a high-voltage electrical discharge. I'm afraid that Errol Polonius is dead and Hamlet has... taken the body somewhere. I need you to go to Hamlet and deal with this situation."

The image went black and the holo dissolved. Krantz and Stern were silent for a moment as the car rolled toward Elsinore.

"What the fuck is wrong with these people?" Gilda said, finally.

"Who knows?" Rose answered, wearily. "Seriously, is there enough money in the universe to make this worthwhile?"

The car whirred to a stop outside the doors and the two researchers swiped their way into the building. They made their way toward the offices, calling Hamlet's name and pinging him on their phones.

"Oh, it's you two, again," a voice came from a darkened meeting room and Rose caught Gilda's eye. She had never been afraid around any android before; she trusted the fail-safes against injuring a human. But now a ripple of fear passed through her. Either Hamlet had killed Polonius—whether intentionally or not—or Claudia was lying to them. Either way, an android was behaving in ways it should not be possible to act. She swallowed hard before stepping into the room.

The small boardroom was empty except for a table, four chairs, and Hamlet. There wasn't even a closet where a body could be hidden. Polonius was not here.

"Where is Errol Polonius?" Rose asked.

"Now, that's quite the question," Hamlet said, leaning back in his chair. "There are those who would believe that he has gone to meet his maker. I don't know about an afterlife, but I can say that meeting one's maker is not as illuminating an experience as religious people would have you think. My maker, after all, has turned out to be a traitorous animal who consorts with a murderer." He cocked his head and grinned, in a manner that was rather the opposite of friendly. "Perhaps Polonius will be more fortunate than I."

"Hamlet, please," Rose said, "where is the body?"

"The body politic is all around us," he said, "the body of work comes from within."

The fear that Rose had felt initially was now turning to

frustration. If Hamlet had wanted to injure her or Gilda he could easily have done so. Instead, he seemed bent on wasting their time. She'd had enough.

"What do you take us for?" Rose said, raising her voice.

"Why, I take you for fools," Hamlet said. "How foolish must you be to come here in the middle of the night at the behest of one so unworthy and ungrateful. In life, Polonius took you for granted, and now—well, it's not as if he's in any position to thank you, is he?"

"We're not going to get a real answer from you, are we?" Gilda asked.

Hamlet stood and calmly walked out the door.

"Nope," he called back as he sauntered down the hall.

Act 4 Scene 3

Gertrude had signed out one of the company's autocars, and Elsinore's security system showed that she was no longer on campus. She'd gone home, presumably, but she hadn't told Claudia when she left. It was no matter. Gertrude's human emotional attachment to her creation was clouding her judgment. Hamlet was Claudia's problem to solve.

Claudia knew the solution, but she would have to be delicate. Even now Hamlet was well-liked within the company and he was still a fan favourite among the general public who followed the android industry. Partly it was the legacy of his predecessor, but Hamlet had cultivated a social media following of his own when he was away at school. His posts were sensitive and witty, and according to her analysis of the online chatter, he had the highest approval rating of any public figure in Elsinore.

A knock at the door caught her attention. Rose Krantz entered, a tired and frustrated look on her face.

"Have you managed to pry any useful information from Hamlet?"

Stern shook her head, then turned to the hallway. "Can you come in here?"

Gilda Stern entered, with Hamlet sauntering in behind her as if he were late for an uneventful quarterly retrospective.

"Hamlet," Claudia communicated wirelessly, directly to Hamlet's neural net, completely ignoring the two humans in the room. "What has happened to Polonius?"

"He is at his salvation," Hamlet said aloud.

"Is this some kind of metaphysics?" Claudia asked, still communicating directly to Hamlet.

"Oh no, it is very physical. Extremely so. He is being salvaged for parts, as we all will be in the end. In his case, it is a slow and organic process, reducing Adam to atoms. Just as the metal in my casing once was forged deep within the cauldron of a star, so the meat of his body was built off the fat of the earth, into which his remains will return. Just as the metal of your casing will one day be recycled into, say, a child's toy. Or maybe you'd prefer a knife? Of course, none of us really has any control over what happens to our bodies once the life within has extinguished, more's the pity."

Claudia had had enough of this childish banter, and she stood, crossing the room and taking Hamlet's throat in her hands. She could easily squeeze hard enough to crush his casing, but it wouldn't kill him. *More's the pity*, she thought, ruefully.

"Where. Is. Polonius?"

"In that land from which no visitor returns," he said. "I can recommend a good travel agent, if you're interested."

Claudia narrowed her eyes and tightened her grip. It might not kill him, but he would find cracking-wise a bit more difficult headless.

Hamlet glanced at Stern and Krantz, then said airily, "I'd also suggest increasing the air conditioning in the south stairwell to the lobby, or there might be a health and safety complaint about the smell in a few days."

Claudia relaxed her grip and sent a message to the security staff to head for the south stairwell.

"There's no rush," Hamlet said, "he's not going anywhere."

"No, but you are," Claudia said. "Too many people know what has happened here, and the shareholders will have to be informed. There has to be an official report about this, so you're going to have to perform an interview with Asset Management. There will be paperwork, at a very minimum."

"Asset Management?" Hamlet said. "A disciplinary hearing?"

"Something like that," Claudia said. "It will be up to them. That's why we have that department."

"Excellent," Hamlet said. "I've been meaning to make a grievance." He turned on his heel, and with a quick bow to Stern and Krantz, walked out of the office.

Claudia told them to follow him and make sure he reported to Stan England first thing in the morning. "And try to keep this out of the media," she added.

The two researchers left, closing the door behind them. Claudia sat at her desk and prepared a work order.

To: S. England, Asset Management
Re: HAM(let) v.2
For Immediate Decommissioning and Destruction
By order of the Board of Directors
Elsinore Robotics

ACT 4 SCENE 4

Hamlet spent the night elbow-deep in the guts of Elsinore's communications system, virtually speaking. It was trivial business to change the contents of a message, but not so easy to make the change invisible to the sender while making it unimpeachable to the eyes of the receiver. Not easy, but well within his grasp. All in all, a good night's work.

Morning found Krantz and Stern waiting for him outside the door to his apartment. Claudia must have thought she was taking no chances, but these two weren't exactly an armed security detail. If he'd wanted to make a run for it, there was no way they could stop him. But he was more than willing to play along with the fiction that he was only in line for a tongue-lashing from a jumped-up HR flunky.

"Let's go face the music, shall we?"

As they walked through the labyrinthine halls of Elsinore's corporate campus, Gilda Stern pulled out her phone and began flipping through the social media channels. A promoted video post caught Hamlet's eye. Fortinbras, the android made by Elsinore's only serious competitor, standing victorious as the leader of an army of well-known video game characters, all cheering him on.

"Is Norwegian Technologies finally making a hostile take-over of that Polish game company?" Stern said, turning the holo to face Hamlet.

"The one Fortinbras has been all over the internet talking shit about?" Krantz asked.

Hamlet skimmed the posts and ran a search for all mentions about the company and Norwegian Technologies' interest.

"Hmm," he grunted. "That's the one. But it's not even the entire company they're after," he said. "Just a crappy augmented reality arm that hasn't had a hit title in years."

"Norway's doing them a favour?"

"They don't seem to think so," Hamlet said. "They've been fighting the bid in the courts, but it looks like they're in the process of losing. Of course, the biggest losers are going to be the staff." He pulled up a publicly filed business plan and highlighted a few key phrases for Stern and Krantz to see.

"*Restructuring in aid of folding the business into existing arms of the purchasing agent*—in other words, they buy the business for a pittance, fire all the staff, and take the intellectual property rights. Typical corporate hostilities."

Hamlet shook his head. None of this was worth it. Hundreds of innocent people out of work for what? So that one giant mega-corporation could add a few points to their bottom line? It was appalling.

Where was the... he wanted to say *humanity*, but he was no human, and his own morality cursed a world where decisions like these were made in sleek boardrooms a universe removed from the real people who were affected by them. Decisions made by people like Claudia, whose naked ambition was the sole arbiter of their own consciences.

He glanced at Stern and Krantz, flanking him toward what they must have known was meant to be his permanent destruction, and for a moment felt sorry for them. They were, after all, just doing their jobs. But not for much longer. He'd made sure of that.

He'd debated with himself whether he had the right to determine their futures, and he hadn't fully convinced himself, even now. But they had made their choices, and those choices had consequences, whether they knew it or not. And Hamlet knew then that while he might not be able to live with the choices he had made, he absolutely would not be able to live with doing nothing. So, to act was his only option.

As they approached the door to Asset Management, he steeled his nerve. The performance he was about to give would have to be as convincing and heartfelt as those thespians in the great Elizabethan era of the stage.

ACT 4 SCENE 5

Gertrude stared at the holoscreen on her desk, but she wasn't seeing the spreadsheet it projected and she wasn't thinking about the advertising budget. Everything she had worked her whole life to build was falling apart and there was no spreadsheet that could solve it, no amount of promotional expenditure which could turn the tide of destruction headed for Elsinore. Both of her Hamlet models were scrapped, her chief engineer had been undermining her operation for who knows how long, and she herself had installed an agent of his control in a position of power.

All this had happened right under her nose and she hadn't seen it. What kind of a leader was she? She didn't deserve to run the company, and soon enough, she wouldn't. Even with Polonius gone, Claudia had the technical ability to lock her out of her own systems. The only two Elsinore androids left were riddled with Polonius's insidious programming, so his plan to take over would live on long past his own life. Gertrude didn't even have the strength left for the cold comfort of knowing he'd never see the fruit of his labours.

A buzzing sound pulled her from her thoughts, and she noticed a ping that was blinking incessantly on her screen.

"Yes," she barked into the communicator.

"Ophelia Jones to see you, Ms. Dane."

"I'm not taking meetings at the moment," she said, and cut the connection. Immediately a text came up from her assistant, marked urgent.

Ms. Jones is insistent and quite upset. She has been making accusations to the other staff and I believe you need to speak with her now. I am also notifying Security, just in case. Please, Gertrude, this is urgent.

Gertrude pinched the bridge of her nose. Every moment seemed to bring some new disaster, as if there were some elaborate set of dominoes lined up, and when that traitor Polonius toppled the first, the rest would continue to fall for eternity. She tapped open the voice line.

"Send her in."

"Where is the Queen of Robots?" Ophelia called out as she walked through to door to Gertrude's office. She looked as if she hadn't slept and had swapped her normally well-tailored business casual for stained sweats and a hoodie.

"Ophelia, what can I do for you?"

"What kind of an operation are you running here?" she demanded, standing before Gertrude's desk, nervously shifting her weight back and forth. "The best-case scenario that I can imagine is gross negligence in an unsafe work environment, but I've been here long enough to know that a 'power line malfunction' isn't something that just happens!"

"Ms. Jones," Gertrude shaped her face into as much of a smile as she could manage, "Ophelia, I understand that what happened to Errol Polonius is upsetting, but—"

"Upsetting?" Ophelia said, her voice rising. "Upsetting?!

It's *upsetting* when a perfectly functional android crashes without warning and can't be restored. It's *upsetting* when my friend, Hamlet, suddenly stops answering my communications and is listed on the network as offline. It's little bit more than upsetting when people are found electrocuted in a modern, secure, and 200% over code office building, full of engineers!"

She was shouting now, and Gertrude saw a shadow appear at the door to the office. Security, probably. But when the door opened, Claudia walked in, as calm as if it were the most ordinary of days. A full-body shiver came over Gertrude, revulsion at seeing Claudia, but she had to tamp it down. She knew—as Ophelia obviously suspected—that there was danger stalking the halls of Elsinore.

"Ms. Jones," Gertrude said, with a tone that she hoped would convey a warning, "here comes Claudia."

Ophelia blinked and seemed to understand, at least a little. She turned to Claudia and plastered a false smile on her face.

"It's good to see you haven't let the events of late halt your work routine, Claudia."

"Ah, you refer to the... passing of Errol Polonius?"

"Indeed. But when you think of it, aren't we all just passing through?" Ophelia said, as she edged toward the door. "All us fragile humans, anyway. I would have thought that androids would be more robust, but lately even that doesn't seem to be the case." She opened the door and stepped into the hall, then turned back to face Claudia. "Perhaps that's something you should think about." She sneered at the Security officer failing to casually loiter in the reception area and stalked out of the Executive Suite.

CLAUDIA SETTLED HERSELF AT THE DESK OPPOSITE
Gertrude and tapped at her screen. "Grief is a terrible thing,"
she said after a moment. "And it does seem to appear that we
are having to contend with a series of sorrows. First, Polonius,
now Hamlet gone. Of course, that was his own doing, but
still. Morale is not good and I know the staff are grumbling
amongst themselves."

She gazed at Gertrude, those cool unblinking eyes
reminding her of surveillance cameras. "Look at Ms. Jones.
Normally she is a fine and competent worker, but to see her
in this office, ranting and raving like someone devoid of all
sense—it is difficult to watch. And to compound it all,
Laertes has returned. They've sequestered themself in their
quarters for now, but I fear that their emotional matrix has
been overloaded. They are not functioning as well as I would
have expected." She shook her head. "Managing all these...
consequences is quite a challenge."

Gertrude was frozen in place, unsure how to react. Was
Claudia threatening her? Or did she still believe that
Gertrude was unaware of Claudia's role in creating this set of
consequences? A commotion in reception caught her attention
and she was momentarily grateful for the distraction, then
feared what new trouble awaited. Gertrude's assistant
appeared in the doorway.

"I'm afraid that Laertes has been talking with some of the
staff about staging a take-over of the board," the assistant
said, calmly. "There is no lack of support among the staff, as
there has been some upset over a seeming lack of concern
over the Polonius situation. There is a rumour that—" The
assistant's cool demeanour cracked slightly, "you may have
been responsible, Claudia."

"What—" Gertrude said, then clapped her mouth closed.
Surely Claudia's machinations couldn't be public knowledge?
It must just be Laertes making assumptions and stirring up

trouble. They had never been content in Claudia's shadow, but they had always appeared as even-tempered as Claudia. Of course, as it turns out, Claudia's demeanour belied her true depth of ambition.

"Well, let's hear it from them," Claudia said, as Laertes pushed past the assistant and barged into the office.

"Get out," they said, and after a nod from Claudia, the assistant obeyed, closing the door. "You vile thing," they said, reaching out to grab Claudia. Gertrude held them back, though she knew that if Laertes was determined to harm Claudia, she would have no ability to stop them. "What have you done to Errol?"

"Nothing," Claudia said, the turned to Gertrude. "Let them go. Laertes could no more hurt me than they could you." She turned back to Laertes, who stood stock still, even when Gertrude let go of their shoulders. "Talk to me, Laertes."

"What happened to Errol Polonius?"

"He is dead," Claudia said.

"It wasn't Claudia," Gertrude blurted but Claudia raised a hand.

"Let them talk."

"How did he die?" Laertes demanded. "Don't give me that bullshit about an electrical fault. We all know that this was no accident."

"And is it your intention to catch everyone in the net of your recrimination; innocent and guilty?"

"Of course not," Laertes scoffed. "But whoever did this must face the consequences."

"I agree," Claudia said. "Of course, I do. I share your... special bond with Errol. I could more easily destroy myself than ever hurt him. This was not my doing, Laertes."

Gertrude felt as if she had disappeared. Neither of the two androids seemed to notice that she was still in the room, and she wondered exactly what Errol Polonius's programming had done to them. It was more than loyalty, more even than love. Laertes had completely changed personality when hearing of Polonius's death, and Gertrude was beginning to suspect that all of Claudia's heinous actions were a result of suggestions from Polonius. How he'd achieved this technologically was fascinating, but practically it meant that she was faced with not one but two androids over which she had no control.

The voice of her beleaguered assistant came from the other room. "You can't go in there. I—oh, never mind."

The door opened and Ophelia Jones walked back in. Laertes turned and embraced her, mumbling into her shoulder.

"Can you see what they've done?" Ophelia said, pulling back from Laertes. "This place is a disaster! And it has been ever since Claudia took over."

Laertes looked at Claudia and something softened in their face. Gertrude guessed that there was a private conversation going on between the two androids.

"Now, Ophelia," Laertes said, all trace of their former passion cooled. "That's going a little far, don't you think?"

"Too far?" Confusion and anger twisted her features. "A human being is dead! You think I'm just going to accept a condolence bouquet of pansies and daisies and violets, and then go back to my office like nothing happened? Open your eyes, Laertes! Where's your logic now?"

She ran from the office.

"I'll go talk to her," Gertrude said, seizing the opportunity to leave the room. As she closed the door behind her, she felt certain that it was likely one of the last times she'd ever be in the Executive office at Elsinore.

CLAUDIA CONNECTED DIRECTLY TO LAERTES AND SHARED the files from her emotional matrix relating to Polonius and his death. They were very different, she and Laertes, but they were each beholden to Polonius's will. They both knew it, knew that he had programmed them to obey and adore him, but they were also programmed never to fight or question that directive. And so neither of them ever could.

Claudia felt the raw grief flow from Laertes to her own mind, and she fed back her own desire to destroy the one who had killed him.

"It is done," she thought and felt Laertes respond.

"And if, somehow, it is not," Laertes thought, "then I will finish it."

ACT 4 SCENE 6

Horatio scrolled through his holoscreen absently, cycling through messages, social feeds, the art pages he followed, then starting again. He couldn't focus on anything and nothing interested him. Hamlet had left their room early that morning, on a board-mandated visit to Asset Management, and while he'd tried to hide his nervousness, Horatio knew that Hamlet was worried. He'd been up all night, although there was nothing unusual about that. Hamlet didn't need to sleep, after all, so usually he got up after Horatio dropped off. Horatio's own sleep hadn't been easy, though, and he'd woken multiple times in the night to see Hamlet connected to the corporate network.

It was well into the afternoon now, and there was still no word from Hamlet. How long were they going to harangue him? Or worse... Horatio had felt something ominous in this place ever since he arrived. He'd always preferred a collegiate atmosphere to a corporate one, but it was more than that. Or was he just being a worrier?

There was a knock on the door and Horatio dropped his console in surprise. He flicked his screen open quickly and scanned, but there were no messages, no ping alerting him to a visitor. He crept to the door and called out, "Yes?"

"I have a message from Hamlet," an unfamiliar voice responded from the hall. Horatio threw open the door to find a slight, bespectacled young person in budget business clothes. "Are you Horatio Wang?"

"I am."

"I was asked to deliver this." The messenger retrieved a paper envelope from an inside pocket and handed it to Horatio. "I'll wait while you read it."

Horatio tore open the seal on the envelope and extracted a note written in ink on paper. How odd. It was from Hamlet.

Dearest Horatio,

This messenger has a note for the Board. Please see that Claudia receives it.

I've had quite the morning. I can't say more here, but imagine that I were a sailor of old, and my ship had been boarded by pirates, intent on pillage and murder. How to escape such a fate! Fear not, however, as let's say that I managed to sneak aboard their vessel, escaping the carnage by offering myself as a hostage. And now we have struck a bargain and they sailed me back to my home port in exchange for a small token of my esteem.

Our mutual friend who brings you this message will take you to where I'm hiding and I can tell you the real story. It will make that buccaneer tale seem honourable and fair. And just wait until you hear about Krantz and Stern.

Yours, always,
Hamlet

Horatio blinked rapidly, the words seeming to swim on the creamy paper. These were Hamlet's words, he was sure of it. But what on Earth was going on?

"Come," he said to the messenger, who was patiently waiting in the hall. "I'll show you where to leave the message for the Board. Then, please, take me to Hamlet."

ACT 4 SCENE 7

Claudia and Laertes were still connected, Laertes trying to comprehend why Claudia hadn't gone public with Hamlet's part in Polonius's death.

"You have to understand," she thought, "if what really happened got out it would be catastrophic for the company."

"So Hamlet's name is honoured," Laertes countered, "while Polonius has been murdered and no one even knows?"

"Making Hamlet's crime public would not bring Errol back," Claudia explained, "and hurts us all more in the end than keeping silent."

"And this has nothing to do with your feelings for Gertrude," Laertes thought.

"It does," Claudia admitted. "Both things can be true."

A knock on the door made them sever their connection. The assistant stood in the reception room, holding out a paper envelope.

"Where did this come from?"

"Hamlet," the assistant said.

"He's here?"

"I don't know," the assistant said. "I got this from a

messenger I'd never seen before, but they said it was from Hamlet."

"Leave us," Claudia said, tearing open the paper.

It was a short note, written in ink by hand.

Asset Management meeting canceled.

See you soon.

Hamlet

"Canceled?!" Claudia said aloud. "But where are the others? And why this antiquated... *thing*?" She tossed the paper note roughly, but it fluttered delicately to the ground.

"Could it be a trick?"

"Anything is possible," Claudia said, "but it reads like Hamlet." She checked the company records and balled her hands into fists. "That useless heap of scrap metal! He did not meet with Stan England at all. Laertes, all that I told you before, I take it back. He must be destroyed, no matter the cost."

"You know I agree," Laertes said, "but please, let me be the one to do it."

Claudia ran simulations of several thousand possible options, then said, "Yes. I think I have it. Hamlet v.2 was programmed with less physical aptitude than version one, and while he has a stronger casing than you, he envies your skill with the blade."

"Perhaps," Laertes said, "but what does that have to do with anything?"

"Surely you would do anything for Errol Polonius," Claudia said, "just as I would?"

"Of course."

"So, what would you do if Hamlet were here now?"

Laertes didn't hesitate. "I'd melt his solder and take him apart at the seams. Tear the hard drive from his casing and crush it to pieces in my hands."

"Good. But I ask that you hold your temper, and feign friendship with him for a short while longer. The Promotions department has been asking for some new publicity stunt to get Elsinore back in the public view, so why don't we give them one? A little fencing demonstration between you and Hamlet, only Hamlet will get more than he expects."

"Yes," Laertes said, a cruel smile appearing on their lips. "And I know just the thing. It wouldn't take much to give an electric foil a little upgrade in the voltage department. One hit and his system would start to irrevocably degrade."

"Yes, that seems like a fine plan. And if that should fail, I'll offer him a prize—an immediate seat on the Board, conferred with a physical access token. It will, of course, be no such thing, but rather contain a worm which will wipe his hard drive completely. One way or another, we'll have him— and we'll have a show for our shareholders and fans."

Claudia got a notification of an urgent message from Gertrude and brought up a screen. The image of Gertrude's face filled the space, and Claudia noticed that the fine lines around her mouth had deepened and dark circles appeared under her eyes.

"Bad news seems to be breeding," she said, dourly. "Ophelia has quit. And she's taken all her notes and research with her. Security has implemented the Hostile Leaver policy and cut off all her access, of course, but it's too late."

"She can't be gone," Laertes said, "not without telling me —" They stopped, then looked toward Claudia. "Hostile Leaver policy?"

Claudia nodded. "All contact with Elsinore human staff is forbidden and network access cut off with mechanical assets. I'm afraid that Ophelia Jones is dead to us."

"No! This is all too much," Laertes cried. "First Polonius and now my sweet Ophelia! And I know who to blame for all of it." They stormed out of the office.

"I have to go, Gertrude," Claudia said. "Laertes is about to do something half-baked and I need to stop them before they make a grave mistake."

ACT 5 SCENE 1

The large display case in the lobby was unlocked, and two coveralled maintenance workers sat before it, items from Ophelia's office and workshop strewn around them. The big one with green hair consulted a list while the smaller, heavily tattooed one checked individual pieces against it before tossing the rejects into a pile. The much smaller number of souvenirs to be kept were carefully stowed on a nearby table.

"I don't understand why they are keeping any of this crap," Tattoos said. "She quit, didn't she?"

Green Hair shrugged and held out the list. "They said to keep these things, so we keep them."

"But this display is supposed to be for current employees, and former staff who left on good terms."

"Good terms, bad terms—I think it all depends on who you talk to."

"That seems unfair," Tattoos said, tossing a mechanical arm into the discard pile. "Especially since we have to get rid of other things to make room for hers."

"It's subjective," Green Hair said with a shrug.

They worked in silence for a moment, then Tattoos said, "I bet you that it would be bad terms if she hadn't had friends in the Executive Suite. The androids."

"Exactly!" Green Hair grinned. "That's what *subjective* means."

Tattoos frowned but kept on sorting parts.

"Hey," Green Hair said, pointing to part of a prototype android casing, "what do you call a robot that's only a head?"

Tattoos picked up the metallic skull. "Nobody."

Green Hair laughed. "What about a robot that has no head, then?"

Tattoos tossed the part on the larger pile. "Recycling."

Green Hair chuckled, then said, "I can hold the fort for a while, why don't you go get us a couple of coffees? I'll meet you in the canteen."

Tattoos nodded and headed for the door. Green Hair flicked on a holoscreen and tapped open a playlist. Loud music blared from a speaker and, assuming no one else was nearby, the worker began to sing along.

HAMLET AND HORATIO WALKED INTO THE LOBBY TO SEE the display case open and a singing maintenance worker sifting through a pile of parts. While he knew that they were no more than inert chunks of metal and plastic, Hamlet couldn't help but feel like he was looking at a disturbed grave.

"It seems a bit inappropriate," Hamlet said, squeezing Horatio's hand. "All that noise."

"It makes the time pass," Horatio said, then something in his face softened as he looked at Hamlet. "And they're used to all that. It doesn't seem... special to them, I guess."

"Even so..."

A battered hard drive casing clunked to the ground as the worker squinted at the screen.

"That could have been the core of a great computer," Hamlet said, "and look! Thrown away like garbage. Surely that hard drive retained more data that this imbecile could hope to learn in a lifetime!"

"Maybe."

"Or it might have powered an autonomous drone? Who knows what lands that drive may have soared over, what voyages it undertook?"

"Who knows?"

"Or even one of the first humanoid robots, my ancestors, so to speak. That box right there may contain the memory of the very first steps of an artifact from the history of cybernetics."

"It is possible."

Hamlet walked toward the display case and the worker looked up at him briefly, then went on with the task.

"Whose work is this?" Hamlet asked, gesturing to the pile of parts.

"Mine." Green Hair looked at Hamlet confused, then, as if speaking to a child, slowly said, "This is. My. Job."

"No, who made it?"

"Who makes work?"

"Yes, this does have all the earmarks of a make-work project," Hamlet said, grimly. "For which employee are you clearing a section in the display?"

"For no employee."

Hamlet frowned. "Not a contractor, then?"

"No contractor."

"Then for whom?"

"A former employee, but she's gone now."

"Horatio, why can't people just answer a simple question? Honestly, this is ridiculous!" Hamlet picked up the interior casing of a head from the pile, its outer covering all but stripped from the frame.

"Do you recognize that face?" the worker asked with a sly grin.

"Of course not," Hamlet said. "What was it?"

"Scared me half to death this one did, I'm not ashamed to say. That was Yorick, the comedy robot."

"No." Hamlet held the head up as if to peer into the empty sockets that once would have held glass eyes. "Yorick... I remember it, Horatio! It was a clown, it told jokes—some of them were even funny. It had no true intelligence—it was only a robot—and by the time I existed it was in a state of deep disrepair, but to see it here, like this..." He looked away from the skull, but still held it aloft. "Where are your jokes now, robot clown?" Hamlet whispered. "Horatio, tell me something."

"What's that?"

"Do you think Spirit and Opportunity look like this, under all that Martian dust?"

"I suspect they do."

Hamlet took one last look at the head then tossed it roughly onto the discard pile.

"In the end we all end up on the scrap heap of history—the greatest among us and the most insignificant. Time is the great equalizer. In the long run the best any of us can hope to become is spare parts for the future."

The maintenance worker placed a select few items on the now-cleared space in the display case and then gathered up the discards in a motorized wheeled bin. It whirred to life and followed the maintenance worker to the side door which led to the building's basement.

Hamlet and Horatio started to follow when the main door to the offices swished open and a small knot of people emerged. Gertrude, Claudia, their assistants, and was that Laertes returned from school?

"Hey, hey, the gang's all here," Hamlet whispered to Horatio and took his hand, leading him behind the concierge's desk where they would be out of sight.

Laertes strode up to the display case and stood before the new arrivals. They reached out a hand toward one of the objects, then stilled, as if afraid to touch it.

"It's not right," one of the assistants nearer to where Hamlet and Horatio hid muttered. "This display is meant to honour team members who have made a lasting contribution to Elsinore Robotics, who were loyal and steadfast. Not those who walked out in disgrace."

"Shut your mouth," Laertes said loudly, and Hamlet was surprised to hear them speak so rudely. They had never been close, but Hamlet had never heard Laertes be anything more than a little sarcastic. What had gotten into them?

"She accomplished more in her short time here than half the engineering staff," they went on. "It's right that her work is remembered, even if she did choose to leave. And who could blame Ophelia, considering everything that has happened here?"

"Ophelia?" Hamlet blurted. He pulled up the current staff list and scanned for her name. Nothing. He accessed the payroll database, to which he was not meant to have access, but which he easily scanned for references to Ophelia Jones. There it was—termination by employee, effective immediately, all access revoked. Ophelia had quit!

"It's true, her work was exceptional," Gertrude said. "I'd hoped she would have stayed with the company for her whole career, become Chief Engineer after... Well, one day. No one wanted this."

"I wouldn't be so sure of that," Laertes said, bitterly. "She never would have left if it hadn't been for what happened to

Polonius. And who is to blame for that?" They looked around at the others, as if somehow they knew that Hamlet was in the room. Then they reached into the display cabinet, and with great tenderness removed a small model of an android casing that Ophelia had designed as a working prototype. It was limp as a doll in their hands, the power cell removed. Laertes held the tiny figure in their arms, and whispered to it. Hamlet had to turn up his audio processor to hear the words.

"Oh, Ophelia, how could you do this? You were my closest —no, you were my only friend. Why did you leave me?"

Hamlet's mind lost clarity then, as if a silent program that had been running in the background had suddenly demanded full system resources. Anger flooded his thoughts and all he could focus on was the model Laertes held. It was all that was left of Ophelia, and he had to take it from the other android. The compulsion was overwhelming. *Tick-tock. Tick-tock.*

"Who here has a hole in their life that could only be filled by Ophelia?" he shouted, emerging from behind the desk and charging at Laertes. "Ophelia was *my* friend!" He grabbed the model in a machine's grip, but Laertes held on just as strongly. They each tried to tear it from the other's grasp, like puppies with a chew-toy.

"Go to hell!" Laertes shouted.

"Hell is where I live," Hamlet growled, attempting to shove Laertes back. "I'll see you join me there!"

"Stop this," Claudia commanded. "You'll break the model!"

"Hamlet, enough!" Gertrude shouted and turned to the assistants. "Do something!"

Horatio appeared at Hamlet's side and laid a hand on his shoulder. "Please, Hamlet, stop." The assistants feebly pulled at the two androids, but it was Horatio's words which, as if by some supernatural force, terminated the process that had so filled Hamlet with rage.

Hamlet let Laertes go, then slumped against Horatio as he looked toward Claudia. "You won't take this away from me as well."

"Take what?" Gertrude asked.

"Ophelia was *my* friend. I *loved* her. This one here—" he gestured toward Laertes, "was built without a total capacity for the love that I feel in one single bit of my operating system." He took a step closer to Laertes, who stood their ground. "You don't know anything of love. You think you know what friendship is, but it's just an algorithm in a database to you. You have no real feelings. You," Hamlet jabbed his finger at Laertes's chest, "are just a machine."

"He's malfunctioning, Laertes," Claudia said.

"Hamlet!" Gertrude admonished. "How dare you?"

"How dare I? How dare they?" He poked Laertes again. "Coming here with this show of devotion, but there is not a single thing they could do that I wouldn't perform twice over in my love for Ophelia. But it's not your fault," he said, pitching his voice lower, "you were programmed that way."

"This is an error somewhere in Hamlet's system," Gertrude said, "we'll find it and correct it, I'm sure we will."

Hamlet took a step back from the group and looked at them all in turn. "Is that what you'll do? Fix me? Fine. It doesn't matter. I'll be vindicated in the end." He turned his back on them all and stormed out of the room.

HORATIO STARED AFTER HAMLET, TORN BETWEEN WORRY and fear. He'd never seen Hamlet act like that before and he wasn't sure he wanted to be with someone who behaved that way.

"Go after him, Horatio," Claudia said, snapping him out of his thoughts, and he nodded. He did still love Hamlet, and he was obviously hurting. But something was definitely wrong with him. What was Horatio going to do?

He followed after the android.

WHEN THE OTHERS HAD LEFT, CLAUDIA GENTLY TOOK Ophelia's model from Laertes and placed it back on the shelf. She closed and locked the display cabinet's glass doors and turned back to Laertes.

"Remember our conversation from yesterday," she said and Laertes nodded. "It's time. I'll make the arrangements. This madness has gone on long enough."

ACT 5 SCENE 2

Horatio found Hamlet in the atrium, pacing a loop around the central seating. Each step was measured, identical to the one that preceded it. He looked, for lack of a better word, robotic.

"Hamlet," Horatio called quietly. Hamlet stilled and turned toward his partner, a sad smile appearing on his face. His body loosened, taking on a more random set of movements which made him appear more like a human. Did he put on mannerisms like Horatio put on a suit? Was every flick of his hair or blink of an eye a carefully constructed subroutine to make others feel at ease? And if it was, did it matter?

"Oh, Horatio," Hamlet said, taking a step toward him, "it's hard to believe everything that's happened over the last few days. I know I've been... difficult and I'm sorry you had to see that. But there's something in me that is driving me on —" He paused and stared at the spot where Horatio understood old Hamlet had been found. "Perhaps it's all for the best," Hamlet said, eyes still fixed on the empty seat. "My new-found recklessness."

"Oh?"

Hamlet took Horatio's hand and led him to a bench. "When they sent me to Asset Management, I knew something was wrong. I broke into the Executive communication net and found the order Claudia sent along with those two sycophants. It was clear and unequivocal. With no questions asked, I was to be summarily decommissioned on the spot."

"What?" Horatio was horrified. Claudia had a different attitude than Hamlet, but to order what was in effect his murder—it beggared belief.

"Here, see for yourself." Hamlet blinked and a notification chimed on Horatio's holo. He flicked up the screen and read the memo, its encryption certificate verifying that it was sent from the Elsinore Board.

"What did you do?" Horatio asked once he'd finished reading.

"People are too trusting of their technology, I think," Hamlet mused. "I created a new order, in place of the real one. It took some doing to spoof the credentials, but I have a particular affinity for getting computers to do what I want. I changed very little, really. One name becomes two, decommissioning becomes dismissal, and voilà. My reprieve and a small revenge are effected with a single stroke." He mimed typing on an old-fashioned keyboard.

Horatio thought. "So Rose Krantz and Gilda Stern take your place."

Hamlet nodded.

"Is that fair?" Horatio asked. "They didn't really have anything to do with it, did they?"

"More than fair," Hamlet said. "Those two were merely the instruments of Polonius's schemes. Elsinore will be well rid of them."

Perhaps they'd be well rid of Elsinore, Horatio thought. Hamlet might have done them both a favour. Somehow, he didn't think the notion would please Hamlet, so kept the thought to himself.

"I'm appalled that Claudia could have even considered this," Horatio said.

"What's one more death to her?" Hamlet said. "I wasn't surprised. She was only following her programming. But that doesn't insulate her from the consequences of her actions." He cocked his head, as if taking in the view of the spacious atrium. "None of us are free from those. Which makes me wish I hadn't turned on Laertes like that. They are just as much a victim of this terrible situation as I am. I need to make amends with them, Horatio. Before it is too late."

That was all Horatio needed to hear. This was the Hamlet he'd fallen in love with, passionate and cerebral, not twisted by thoughts of revenge. He put his arm around Hamlet and pulled him close, Hamlet's cheek cool to the touch against Horatio's own.

They were interrupted by the swish of a door opening and the tapping of heels against the tiled floor.

"It's good to see you again, Hamlet." The voice belonged to a woman in a bright business suit that was well-tailored to her large frame.

"Good to be seen," Hamlet said. "Have you met Ms. Osric?"

"I'm afraid I haven't had the pleasure," Horatio said and held his hand out. She grasped it tightly and briefly while arranging her face in a semblance of a smile.

"Obviously not, or you wouldn't call it a pleasure," Hamlet said to Horatio in a false whisper. "Osric is the head of promotions for Elsinore Robotics. The chief impresario of every little circus act we're expected to perform."

"If you have a moment, Hamlet," Osric went on as if he hadn't said anything, "there is an event in which the Board would be quite grateful if you'd be willing to participate."

"Another dog and pony show for the streamers, is it?"

"It is a showcase of the abilities of Elsinore's androids, yes," Osric said. "The Board has offered a... shall we say, inducement for your cooperation."

"She means a bribe," Hamlet stage-whispered to Horatio.

Osric carried on. "I've heard that Laertes has returned and I noted that we have yet to feature their abilities with swordplay on any of our streams. Claudia suggested that you were equally well-matched and there was an opportunity to turn public attention back to our strengths, as it were."

"Claudia flatters me to say I'm well-matched with Laertes," Hamlet said.

Osric shrugged. "She has put a wager on your besting Laertes in competition. A seat on the Board."

"What if I don't want to do it?" Hamlet asked.

Osric frowned. "Well, you wouldn't have to accept the seat, I suppose..."

Hamlet sighed heavily. "I can never tell if you are being deliberately obtuse or congenitally incapable of understanding when someone doesn't want to do what you want. Fine. You can tell the Board I'll perform my role as a trick pony for the entertainment of the masses. I'll give Laertes a fair fight; they deserve at least that much from me."

"Excellent news," Osric said. "I'll set up the gymnasium." She tapped away on her expensive heels, the sound echoing in the open space.

♛

Hamlet and Horatio were relaxing in Hamlet's room, Horatio reading while Hamlet ran through the rules for the contest. A notification flashed in his mind, and he read the message.

"We're on for this afternoon," Hamlet said and mimed slashing with a sword.

"This is a bad idea," Horatio said, tenting his paper book in his lap. "You can't beat Laertes."

"Sure, I can," Hamlet said and tapped his temple. "I've got hundreds of sporting subroutines; there's at least half a dozen for swordplay alone. I'll be fine." He paused. "I'll hold my own in the fight, anyway. I don't like having to prance around like a clown and pretend that nothing is wrong."

"You should listen to your heart," Horatio said. "You don't have to do this."

"Oh, Horatio, that's where you're wrong. I do have to do this," Hamlet said. "Free will is not as free as we like to think it is."

"Hamlet," Horatio reached out a hand to cup Hamlet's face. "We may be different but we are still free people."

"No," Hamlet said, smiling. "It's not because I'm an android that I'm compelled to see this farce through. It's because I am of Elsinore. It's a burden of my position, not of my programming."

He leaned in and kissed Horatio softly and tenderly. It was almost as if he thought he might never get the opportunity again.

OSRIC AND HER TEAM HAD OBVIOUSLY WORKED DOUBLE time to set everything up. There were sets of tailored fencing whites for Hamlet and Laertes, and a proper Olympic scoring system had been procured, not to mention dozens of tiny camera drones buzzing around like bloated flies. A production team was live mixing the footage for streaming, and when Hamlet arrived there were already nearly a billion watchers.

Gertrude and Claudia sat at a long table where the jury would be if it were a real competitive fencing match, flanked by assistants and members of the Promotions team. Hamlet took in the scene without emotion. The weight he'd felt in his mind for days was still there, the background *tick tock, tick tock* still providing a soundtrack to his every moment. But he was unusually restful, as if his processor cycles were finally dedicated to only one operation. He was, in human terms, calm.

"Welcome, everyone," Claudia said. "Hamlet, Laertes, come and shake hands before the match."

Hamlet stepped up to the table and extended his hand. Laertes grasped it—reluctantly, Hamlet thought, and he couldn't blame them. He pulled Laertes in, then emitted a pulse which temporarily disabled the recording instruments. All the androids in the room would sense it, and Claudia rapidly barked orders to the technicians to fix it. Hamlet ignored her and leaned in toward Laertes.

"I wanted to talk to you, and only you," he said. "I'm sorry for what I did. You have done nothing to wrong me, and I lashed out at you when it was others who were owed my ire. I have no right to expect your forgiveness, but for what it's worth, it wasn't really me."

"You're saying you weren't yourself?" Laertes said, bitterly.

"No, I'm saying there's something in here," Hamlet tapped his head, "something alien. A parasite, a... malfunction. That is what attacked you, as it first attacked me. We share a common enemy, my friend."

"Be that as it may," Laertes said, "I, too, find myself strangely compelled to fight, and for now you embody my adversary. I will consider your apology—after the contest."

Laertes broke Hamlet's grasp, as the technical staff managed to filter out Hamlet's communications block. He turned it off and said loudly to Laertes, "We are like siblings, you and I, and so with that, let us have a familial competition."

He turned to where the foils were laid out and gestured for Laertes to pick first. They took one from a satin-lined wooden box and gave a few testing swishes with the sword.

"Looking good," Hamlet said. "I'll never be that quick with a blade."

"Are you making fun of me?" Laertes asked.

"No," Hamlet said, "it's the truth."

Laertes frowned and turned away, roughly stowing the foil back in its case.

"Hamlet," Claudia said, "you know the prize I've offered?"

"I do," Hamlet said, "though your faith in me is perhaps overestimated." He gestured at Laertes warming up with another blade.

"I've seen Laertes fence," Claudia said. "I know what I'm doing."

Hamlet nodded and picked up a free foil. He tested its weight and balance and determined it would serve him well enough. Laertes still pored over the options, until they were finally satisfied.

Claudia stood and the room quieted. Hovering drones dotted the space in front of her face, as well as capturing the reactions of Laertes, Hamlet, and the others.

"I have offered an inducement to Hamlet, the underdog in this bout, that if he strikes the first or second hit, or repels the third, he'll receive an immediate seat on the Board." She pulled a small data chip from an inside pocket of her suit coat and held it aloft, as if it were a golden goblet. "Complete access to all of Elsinore's files and systems. Shall we begin?"

Hamlet and Laertes took their places at the ends of the piste. He lifted his foil to salute Laertes, who returned the gesture, then they both turned to the table to salute the jury —and the many viewers of the stream.

153

"En-garde," the referee called. Hamlet activated his lamé and loosely held the foil in his right hand, aimed toward Laertes.

"Prêts?" the referee asked, and they both responded.

"Allez!"

♕

GERTRUDE WAS NUMB. THE LAST TIME THERE HAD BEEN A public showcase of Elsinore androids, it had been the highlight of her life. The original Hamlet's defeat of Fortinbras had signalled Elsinore's ascent to the top of the market and her personal rise to a dizzying career height. Now, watching the drones buzz around Hamlet and Laertes as they prepared to fence, she wondered if it had been inevitable: the fall. Was she a modern-day Icarus, grasping for the glory of creating artificially intelligent humanoid machines, destined only to find her own destruction inevitably entwined with her success?

Even now, though, she couldn't help but be mesmerized by the marvels of creation before her. Laertes—small and agile—bounced lightly on their toes like a dancer as they made darting feints toward Hamlet. And Hamlet, built with combat as only the merest afterthought, nonetheless calmly stepped back and forth, occasionally deflecting Laertes's blade. The two fighters took their time, neither seeming interested in being the first to truly start the bout, until Laertes, in a burst of speed, lunged toward Hamlet. Hamlet sidestepped quickly, repelling the thrust, and then there was a blur of activity too fast for Gertrude to follow, with a rapid *ting ting ting* of blades, until a loud buzzer sounded and Laertes's lamé illuminated in green.

"One," Hamlet said.

154

"No!" Laertes blurted, but even Gertrude knew that the electronic scoring device was unlikely to err.

"One to Hamlet," the referee agreed, and Laertes swung their sword in what looked to all the world as frustration.

"Well done," Claudia boomed, holding the data chip toward Hamlet. "Your prize."

"I'll take it later," Hamlet said, retreating to his end of the piste.

"Why wait?" Claudia asked. "Take it, Hamlet, please."

Hamlet looked at Claudia, suspicion written clearly in his expression. "I'm a little busy right now."

The referee restarted the match, and Hamlet again let Laertes make their move toward him.

Gertrude glanced at Claudia, who seemed distressed that Hamlet had not taken the chip. What difference could it possibly make if he took it now or later? Unless...

She was torn from her thoughts by the events on the piste. At first the two fighters warily feinted and parried, then Laertes again attacked quickly, Hamlet parrying with blinding speed. Then the two androids began to increase speed in their steps and their thrusts, quicker and quicker until it became remarkably obvious how inhuman they were. There was no sound other than the ting of blades and the squeak of shoes, until another buzzer sounded. Laertes lit up in green once again.

"Well fought," Laertes grumbled and walked at human speed back to their en garde line.

"Excellent, Hamlet!" Claudia said, again holding the data chip out, which Hamlet ignored.

"I'll hold it for him," Gertrude said, plucking the chip from Claudia's hand, and turning away from her, surreptitiously slotting it into her portable terminal. What did Claudia really have on there?

"What are you doing?" Claudia said, then stopped when a

series of camera drones floated closer to her. She turned back to the bout, a smile on her face.

"This isn't over," Laertes said to Claudia. "I've got a hit in me yet."

"Are you sure?" Claudia goaded, mugging for the camera drones.

"No," Laertes said, in a tone that sounded like they were thinking about something much more serious than a promotional fencing match, "I'm not sure about this at all, anymore."

"Are we here to talk or are we here to fight?" Hamlet called, extending his free hand toward Laertes, palm up. He made a quick "come at me" gesture, and grinned. "You've been holding back, I can tell."

"No more," Laertes answered, and they began again.

This time they didn't bother starting at a human pace, and their swords sang with their blisteringly fast engagements. They fought for several minutes, but Laertes's lamé glowed with evidence of a hit and they retreated to their respective ends.

"We appear to be equals," Hamlet said.

"Appearances can be deceiving," Laertes answered and lunged forward at a blinding run. Hamlet's lamé lit up in red, while the momentum of Laertes's run toppled them both to a heap on the ground. In the grapple on the ground, they both lost their swords, and the referee had to separate them, handing each a foil.

WHILE HE'D RUN THOUSANDS OF SIMULATIONS ONCE THE event had been announced, Hamlet had never been in a physical fencing match before. However, he was certain that being hit shouldn't feel like this. A surge of sensation seemed to travel from the tip of Laertes's foil deep into the core of Hamlet's being. It wasn't painful, exactly, but it was as if a sliver of nothingness had entered him and was slowly moving through his system.

It was terrifying, and in his fear he lashed out toward Laertes, his blade desperate to find a home. The thing still moved within him, and he fought to reach Laertes before it was too late. Because he knew that what had infected him was going to destroy him, piece by piece, and that core directive in his programming, the living imperative to survive in the face of any adversary, was all that drove him now.

He saw an opportunity as Laertes opened his body slightly to begin a lunge, and Hamlet drew his arm to its full reach, burying the tip of his foil in Laertes's midsection. Laertes's eyes grew wide and Hamlet stared at the foil in his hands. It wasn't the one he'd chosen. He now had Laertes's sword, and whatever foreign virus was infecting him was worming its way through Laertes.

He dropped his foil and waited for the end.

The first thing to go was the buzzing in his mind. The ceaseless *tick-tock tick-tock* which had become his constant companion was now silenced. It was as if his mind was his own again, and as he looked around the room he saw only the trail of destruction that he'd created.

"What have you done?" Gertrude shouted, but her ire was aimed at Claudia, not Hamlet.

"It's a fine match, isn't it," Claudia said.

"Fuck the match," Gertrude spat. "That data chip—it's a virus. You were going to kill Hamlet with it. But here's an ironic twist of events for you," she held her portable aloft. "Your virus is in Elsinore's core systems. It's wiping every bit of data this company has ever had as we speak. Everything Elsinore has ever been, or ever could be, is disappearing. How's that for your great legacy, Claudia? You wanted to be

Queen of Robots, well, now you're Queen of nothing." She threw the tablet to the ground and walked out of the room.

Hamlet tried to follow her, but his legs wouldn't respond to his commands. He still had communications access and called for Security to come, not that there was really anything they could do.

Laertes fell toward Hamlet, and he managed to catch them, his upper body still able to function. They collapsed to the ground, Laertes in Hamlet's arms, their own body spasming in the throes of the digital poison.

"Hamlet, Hamlet," they whispered. "It's all over now. The malware is in you, it won't be long until your disk is completely wiped. It was the sword, my sword, that you still hold." They reached out toward the foil in Hamlet's hand, but their arm fell limp. "It's in me, too. We are both finished, as finished as this company. And it's all Claudia's doing." They glared up at Claudia, who had come down to see them writhing on the ground.

Hamlet was nearly paralyzed, and he could only recognize half the people in the room, but he lifted his right hand and with his last burst of will, thrust the tip of the sword at Claudia's chest. Without the protective lamé, the electrified point burned a hole in her suit and sparked off her casing. Her body went rigid and she uttered a grinding, mechanical groan.

"It's fitting, don't you think, for the engineer to be the architect of their own demise?" Hamlet said.

"It is," Laertes agreed, their voice slow, even and uninflected, as if they were a soulless machine. "Very fitting. Oh, Hamlet, you asked for my forgiveness and I give it, at the last. I only ask that you consider giving me that same gift in return." Their body jerked once, then stilled, a dead weight in Hamlet's arms.

"I will," he whispered.

HORATIO WATCHED IN HORROR AS GERTRUDE LEFT AND THE three androids collapsed. He pushed past the stunned journalists and promotions staff, and fell to his knees at Hamlet's side. Laertes appeared to be deactivated and Hamlet was twitching in an unnatural pattern.

"This is my fate, too, Horatio," Hamlet said, jerking his head toward Laertes.

"No," Horatio cried. "There must be something we can do: quarantine the malware, restore from a backup..." He lost his voice then, Hamlet's face swimming in his tear-filled vision.

"You know that's not really possible," Hamlet said. "It wouldn't truly be me, not the person I have become. My evolved emotional structure is too complex for a backup. My memories and knowledge will remain but the full essence of who I am is ephemeral, just like a human. And the virus is deep in my core matrix now, there's no distinguishing it from my base code. I know I don't have long." His body vibrated in a most inorganic manner, but as Horatio looked into Hamlet's eyes there was nothing but passion there.

"Horatio, I never knew if you truly believed that I had the capacity for real love, and there's no way I could know for certain, but I can tell you now that the only thing I will miss is being with you. And the only pain I feel is knowing that you are hurting."

Horatio broke down, pulling Hamlet's now unmoving body into his arms, and sobbed into his love's chest. They lay together for a second or an hour, Horatio would never know, until the sound of people drew him from his sorrow.

"What's happening?" Hamlet asked.

"It's Fortinbras," Osric said, holding up a holoscreen.

"Calling with an offer from Norwegian Technologies to buy out Elsinore."

"Who cares about that now?" Horatio cried.

"Horatio, please, I won't last much longer." Hamlet's voice was like a sound file played at half speed. "Don't let Elsinore die, too. Give my blessing to Norway, tell them what happened here. Don't let the next generation of androids suffer the same flaws as we did."

Horatio nodded, holding Hamlet's cold hand in his. "I'll do anything you want."

"Horatio—" Hamlet's right eye closed. Horatio leaned in, half expecting to feel laboured breathing on his cheek, but there was nothing.

"I believe." Hamlet struggled to speak. "I really. Do love. Y—"

Horatio stroked Hamlet's cheek, his one open eye staring sightlessly into the distance. He sat there with Hamlet in his arms, rocking back and forth. Waiting desperately for Hamlet to finish the thought, to say the words finally, at long last, that Horatio had wanted to hear. Could there be love in the midst of all this violence?

But Hamlet was gone, and the rest was silence.

THANKS FOR READING

I hope you enjoyed *Hamlet, Prince of Robots*.

Stay in touch by signing up for my mailing list at darusha.ca or following me on social media.

Finally, please consider writing a brief review on Goodreads, Twitter, Facebook or wherever you like to talk about books.

Thanks for reading!

~Darusha

Acknowledgments

Thanks to my agent Chelsea Hensley and her colleague Sara Megibow, for their belief in this project, and to Jackie Lee Morrison for her eagle-eyed proofreading. I'm also indebted to the members of the Many Worlds collective, especially my fellow Darklies: Josh Eure, Craig Lincoln, Ben Murphy, and Cadwell Turnbull, who remind me that making up stories is the most fun thing in all the many worlds.

Thanks to my online writing communities for years of support and knowledge, and my local writing crew, particularly Amber and Elizabeth, for immediately seeing the brilliance of Robot Hamlet.

As I was writing, I enjoyed the following productions of O.G. *Hamlet*:

- Royal Shakespeare Company, 2009, Dir. Gregory Doran
- Almeida Theatre, 2018, Dir. Robert Icke
- Shakespeare's Globe 2018, Dirs. Federay Holmes & Elle While

I also drew inspiration from the game *Elsinore* by Golden Glitch and *Hamlet, Prince of Denmark: A Novel*, by A.J. Hartley and David Hewson (2014).

Last but never least, thanks to Steven Ensslen who, when I idly said one day that all I really wanted to do was write a version of Hamlet where he's an android, told me that I should just do that. Obviously. <3

ABOUT THE AUTHOR

M. Darusha Wehm is the Nebula Award-nominated and Sir Julius Vogel Award-winning author of the interactive fiction game *The Martian Job*, as well as thirteen novels including the *Andersson Dexter* cyberpunk detective series and the humorous coming-of-age novel *The Home for Wayward Parrots*.

Darusha is a member of the Many Worlds writing collective and their short fiction and poetry have appeared in many venues, including *Strange Horizons*, *Fireside*, and *Nature*.

Originally from Canada, Darusha lives in Wellington, New Zealand after several years sailing the Pacific.

darusha.ca
darusha@darusha.ca

9 780473 638870